"You never answered me back once upon a time."

James Hackett glared at her in frustration.

"The type of female I was pretending to be would have been incapable of it. I'm afraid the real me isn't nearly as docile." Her eyes met his candidly and James Hackett's narrowed to a hard blue gleam.

"I've noticed that for some time. You really don't like me very much, do you, Theodora? So what made you stay?"

"Personal feelings never enter into my job," she said. "And you pay me very well. May I go now?"

"Only after you've confirmed our travel arrangements to Portugal—and promised to bring a bikini."

She ignored his last remark. "Just two tickets, Mr. Hackett?"

"That's right, Theodora." He grinned down at her. "Just you and me."

CATHERINE GEORGE was born in Wales, and following her marriage to an engineer, lived eight years in Brazil at a gold mine site, an experience she would later draw upon for her books. It was not until she and her husband returned to England and bought a village post office and general store that she submitted her first book at her husband's encouragement. Now her husband helps manage their household so that Catherine can devote more time to her writing. They have two children, a daughter and a son, who share their mother's love of language and writing.

Books by Catherine George

CATHERINE GEORGE

touch me in the morning

Harlequin Books

TORONTO • NEW YORK • LONDON
AMSTERDAM • PARIS • SYDNEY • HAMBURG
STOCKHOLM • ATHENS • TOKYO • MILAN

Harlequin Presents first edition April 1988
ISBN 0-373-11065-0

Original hardcover edition published in 1987
by Mills & Boon Limited

CHAPTER ONE

THIS double life of hers would just have to stop. She stared at her face in the mirror and groaned. Fatigue smudged her eyes and deepened the hollows under her cheekbones, and her pallor was best described as sepulchral. Even her hair, almost chestnut on a good day, looked drab and dark. You, she informed her reflection, should be out haunting someone.

Yawning, she turned away to bully her tired body into the routine of pouring its unwilling weekend persona into the Monday morning mould that turned out her alter ego; the one who went out to work five days a week to earn her daily bread. And butter. Dazed with sleep, she put coffee to perk, then stood under the shower to wake herself up. Eventually, dressed in prim shirt and brown suit with mannish stripes and matching waistcoat, she buffed up the expensive leather of her sensible shoes and scraped her hair back ruthlessly into a tight pleat. Two cups of coffee later she felt sufficiently restored to tidy her attic 'studio', collect her briefcase and add the final touch to her appearance, her owl-lensed, horn-rimmed spectacles. Miss T. Grace, personal assistant to the eponymous head of Hackett Construction, was ready to depart for her working day.

She went slowly down the three flights of stairs to the ground floor hall of the big Victorian house to find her young landlord, Charlie Cowper, sorting out his tenants' mail on the hall table.

'Hello, Charlie,' she said, smothering another yawn.

''Morning, Theo,' he replied absently, then glanced

up and sprang smartly to attention, a broad grin on his face. 'Whoops—stand by your beds. It's Miss Grace herself this morning.'

'It's too early for all that, Charlie,' said Theo, wincing. 'Any letters for me?'

'One nasty brown window envelope and a nice blue one from your mother.'

She shook her head in mock disapproval. 'Fat chance of a private life in your establishment, Charlie Cowper!'

Charlie grinned unrepentantly as he held the door open for her. 'On the contrary—*you* manage it awfully well, Theo. God knows the rest of us at Willow Lodge yearn to know why you make such a fright of yourself to go out to work every day.'

Theo laughed but avoided a reply as they reached the bustle of rush-hour Chiswick High Road, and her lanky, affable escort, in his dark city suit, shepherded her across the busy thoroughfare with great care. Charlie Cowper had inherited Willow Lodge six months earlier and now occupied the garden flat of the sprawling white house near the river. The rest of the house was divided into pricey apartments occupied by various couples, and for her first two years in the attic Theo herself had shared. But since the departure of her friend, Clare, a year ago to marry the man of her dreams Theo lived alone, finding privacy very necessary for the life she had led of late.

Theo waited while Charlie bought a morning paper, then resumed her progress with him along the crowded pavement, her goal a modern office block in Turnham Green, Charlie's the nearby Underground en route to his bank in the city.

'Funny thing is,' remarked Charlie, 'I was convinced at first that there were two of you up there in the top studio. Sisters or something. It came as rather a shock to discover both of 'em were you, in different guises, as it were.'

'I'm not a double agent, Charlie! I just dress down a bit for work, that's all.'

'Down!' Charlie hooted as they dodged through the crowds, then peered at her more closely as they came together again. 'Seriously, love, the Miss Marple look apart, you do seem a bit peaky this morning. Not ill, are you?'

Theo smiled, touched, and patted his arm. 'No. Just tired. Burning the candle at both ends a bit. By the way, Charlie, aren't you running a bit late this morning? I don't normally have the pleasure of your company at this time of the day.'

'Dental appointment first thing,' he said glumly as they reached the building where Hackett Construction had its being. 'Here you are then, Miss Grace, ma'am. Nose at the ready for the grindstone?'

Theo peered past him, frowning as she saw a familiar figure rapidly approaching them. She snatched her briefcase from Charlie. 'Look out, here's my boss. Must go. 'Bye.'

Charlie shot a look at the formidable figure of J. E. M. Hackett, then swept an unprepared Theo into his arms, bending her back in true Hollywood style as he kissed her in impassioned farewell. 'See you tonight, my darling!' he said loudly in throbbing accents. Then, with an outrageous wink, he released her and sprinted off towards the station.

Cheeks burning, Theo fled across the crowded foyer, horribly conscious of stares from several fascinated onlookers, not least the open-mouthed receptionist, Anita, in her bower of potted greenery. Hot with embarrassment, Theo reached the lift just a split second too late. A long male forefinger beat her own into pressing the button for her floor, and with a sinking heart she found herself closeted with James Hackett as the lift ascended with nerve-jangling lack of speed. A furtive glance at him confirmed that he was staring at her like a man in shock. His hard blue eyes usually registered blank indifference during dealings with his efficient secretary, but at this moment they were thunderstruck.

'Who in the name of God was that, Grace?' he demanded.

'Good morning, Mr Hackett,' said Theo stolidly. 'To whom are you referring?'

He snorted. 'Who do you think? The chap mauling you about on the pavement in full view of half my employees.'

Theo gritted her teeth, deeply thankful that the lift chose to stop at that juncture. 'Just a friend, Mr Hackett,' she said colourlessly, and hastily preceded her employer into the corridor. To her relief he was buttonholed by the senior contracts manager as soon as he emerged, and, with another frowning glance at his secretary, James Hackett went off with him, and Monday morning was under way.

In the sanctuary of her own office Theo dumped her briefcase on the floor and subsided limply into the swivel chair behind her desk. Her exasperation over Charlie Cowper's idea of a joke began to ebb slowly as she concentrated on her routine morning confrontation with the post, extra heavy on Monday as always, and after a while, as she worked swiftly and methodically, she was even able to appreciate the funny side of the incident. She smiled at the thought of the jolt it had given James Hackett, and answered the telephone as it rang for the first time that day.

'He's not here, Anita,' she said in reply to the

receptionist's query. 'Try Mr Arrowsmith's office, or accounts.'

'Will do.' Anita could be heard taking in a deep breath. 'Was that your boyfriend this morning, Miss Grace?'

'Just a friend, Anita.' Fame at last, thought Theo with a grin, and went on dealing letters into trays like playing cards. And to have aroused the interest of the great man himself was achievement indeed, since she knew only too well that if he thought of her at all, which was doubtful, it was probably as an efficient computer with convenient extra accomplishments like diplomacy and coffee-making. Not that the majority of nubile woman-kind held a similar lack of interest in James Hackett—far from it. Women fell for him like ninepins, bowled over by his bulldozer brand of charm. Prizefighter physique allied with a shock of grey-streaked black hair and a hard, handsome face seemed irresistible to most women, except Theodora Grace. To his secretary fell the privilege of coping with his workaday self, the iron hand without the velvet glove, and from her own point of view she was only too glad to leave him to those of her sex sufficiently foolhardy to share his social life.

It was no secret that before Theo's advent James Hackett had contrived to run through a record number of secretaries in a very short time. Although the agency that interviewed her for the job had been guarded as to the reason, Theo had already learned why. She had heard of the vacancy in the first place because the most recent Hackett reject was a friend of Clare's, and, like her predecessors, had made the mistake of nurturing romantic tendencies towards her boss. He, it seemed, made a well-publicised point of never mixing business with pleasure, so the unfortunate lady was out on her ear the moment her sentiments were suspected. She had gone on at venomous length to the deeply interested Clare, telling her that what James Hackett wanted, and deserved, was a purely practical frump who looked like the back end of a bus.

'Which lets you out, snookums,' Clare told Theo, giggling. 'I shouldn't even bother to go along to see this ghastly Hackett person.'

Theo had been unconvinced. 'Now you're off to marry Michael I'll need to earn more money to keep the flat on by myself,' she pointed out thoughtfully. 'This job at Hackett Construction is offering a third more than I get now, and it's in walking distance of Willow Lodge. No more rush-hour claustrophobia in the tube—no fares, either. Bliss!'

'Then your only chance is to cut off a foot of hair, wipe off the make-up and borrow something from your granny to wear for the interview!'

Clare's advice had been meant as a joke, but Theo's eyes had glinted with mischief. Hair pinned back instead of cut, and arrayed in a baggy beige linen suit from the Oxfam shop, Theo had turned up for interview at the appointed hour wearing the large tinted spectacles she used for reading in the sun, and looking like an older, staider caricature of her normal vivid self. To her glee it had worked like a charm. James Hackett, after the most cursory of glances at her dossier, had engaged her on the spot, convinced by her appearance that she was unlikely to embarrass any man, let alone James Hackett, with any unwelcome attentions.

Conceited oaf, thought Theo, slitting open a large envelope with venom. The nerve of him, to be so astounded just because he saw a man kissing her this morning, as though such an occurrence were beyond the bounds of possibility! Her lips tightened. A word in Charlie's ear might be a good thing, too. She could do without incidents like that to start the day in her present state. Or at any time if it came to that.

She sighed heavily. Sometimes she cursed the day Hackett had taken her on. Not that she disliked her work, far from it. The job paid better and extended and stimulated her far more than either of the two she'd had previously. And since she hadn't the slightest inclination towards falling in love with her employer everything would be highly satisfactory if only she were free to be her natural self at work. But she'd started off looking like Whistler's mother, so now she was stuck with it. Blast James Hackett and his towering opinion of his own charms. Of course, she conceded absently, to be fair, if it wasn't for him she would never have met the other man in her life, the one responsible for the circles under her eyes and her lack of sleep. Her honey-coloured eyes softened and grew dreamy behind the owlish spectacles until the buzzer on her desk blasted her out of her reverie.

'Yes, Mr Hackett,' she said crisply.

'Get in here, Grace.'

She gathered up the mail and went through the connecting door into James Hackett's large office. As usual there was a hard hat thrown down on a chair and a pair of muddy boots in a corner, somewhat marring the effect of the antique walnut desk and leather squabbed chairs that were the Hackett choice of executive furnishing. A model of an Algarvean holiday complex stood on a table alongside the desk, and Theo kept her attention on the tiny white houses, swimming pools and tennis courts as she sat down with composure, pencil poised, waiting for the curt, impatient voice to begin its usual gunfire rapid instructions.

Nothing happened, and warily Theo looked up to find the bright blue eyes trained on her as though their owner had never seen her clearly before. Which was probably true. Up to now she'd been as much a piece of office equipment to him as her typewriter or the Telex or any of the computers in the company.

'How long have you been working for me, Grace?' asked James Hackett after an unbearably long interval.

'Just over a year.'

'Where do you live?'

Theo sat straighter, her eyes narrowing. 'In Chiswick.'

'The man kissing you this morning—do you live with *him*?' He leaned back in his swivel chair, rather obviously expecting a prim denial.

'Yes,' replied Theo, with some truth.

The effect on Hackett was both satisfying and insulting. His jaw literally dropped with astonishment, and only the jangle of the telephone recalled him to his usual succinct style as he spoke to the resident engineer on one of the building sites.

Theo studied James Hackett covertly while he was holding forth. Not that she ever thought of him as James. He'd dropped the 'Miss' from her name on the first day; in fact she sometimes wondered if he knew she had another name. In retaliation she always thought of him merely as 'Hackett', a sort of Grand Vizier, who 'hacked and hatcheted and slew till none but he was left'—which, if not precisely true, was not so inaccurate either. The head of Hackett Construction was well known for his intolerance of dead wood, and anyone not up to his idea of competence received short shrift. He was large, with a big frame and wide, heavy shoulders that misled as to his actual height, which was well above six feet. As capable of physical hard labour as any 'brickie' employed on any of his construction sites, James Hackett invariably gave the impression of straining the expensive cloth across the shoulders of his custom-made suits, even while impressing his colleagues with the perspicacity of his agile brain.

The conversation over, Hackett's attention returned to Theo once more. She felt uneasy. No one knew better than she just how astute her employer was, and this morning she was not at all pleased to find him focusing on her as a person for the first time, and all because of Charlie Cowper and his silly practical joke.

'I've just realised I know nothing at all about you,' he remarked, unsettling Theo even more.

'It's all in my records, Mr Hackett.'

'I've never even looked at them. You do your job—admirably—which is my main concern.'

'Quite so. Shall we get on?' suggested Theo. 'The mail is quite heavy today.'

James Hackett shook his head. 'Not so fast. How old are you, Grace?'

'Twenty-four.'

His black brows shot up in unflattering surprise. 'Good God! Is that all?'

Theo decided it was wiser to say nothing in reply. Her employer regarded her with searching blue eyes and frowned.

'Now I come to look at you,' he said, 'you really do look under the weather. Both Ben Arrowsmith and Ken Barrett mentioned how ill you've been looking lately, and I can see why. I've never noticed those dark marks under your eyes before.'

Because you've never looked, thought Theo, and rustled the pages of her notebook significantly. 'I'm perfectly well, Mr Hackett.'

'This friend of yours. Is he responsible for your lack of sleep?' The blue eyes were laughing at her now, and Theo gave him a cool stare and said nothing, and

Hackett suddenly lost interest, abandoning personalities for the matters of the day, to her infinite relief. She was far happier up to her ears in the usual Monday avalanche of work than fending off intimate questions about herself from James Hackett. Her private life was something she kept rigidly separate from her job. No one, not even her family, had yet been allowed an inkling about the secret man in her life, and Hackett would definitely be the last to know if Theo had anything to do with it.

There was no more time that day for introspection. Hackett spent the day in meetings with heads of departments or on the telephone to Portugal, and Theo worked like a machine the whole time, soothing ruffled tempers along the way as people waited in her office for a few minutes of her employer's time. She was forced to delegate some of the more routine work to the typing pool, but even so got through an exhausting amount of it herself, and it was late when the daily uproar finally died down.

Hackett finished signing the letters Theo was waiting for and handed them over, yawning. 'God, what a day.' He eyed her closely as she relieved him of the mail file. 'You look shattered, Grace.'

'No more than usual,' she said pointedly. 'Goodnight, Mr Hackett.'

He frowned as he muttered a response, and Theo could feel his eyes boring into the back of her pinstriped jacket as she closed the door quietly behind her. With a sigh of relief she gathered up her belongings swiftly, anxious to get away before Hackett could emerge from his lair and corner her with any more of his unwelcome questions. His normal indifference was a great deal more preferable to this sudden show of interest. Theo shrugged philosophically as she went down in the lift, assuring herself that his attitude was a one-off. He would, no doubt, have forgotten all about her by now, she decided, and hurried off to buy take-away fried chicken on the way home, knowing very well she was too tired to attempt any form of home cooking after the day she'd just spent.

Before she ate, Theo changed into cotton trousers and a baggy sweater, and made up her eyes and lips until she felt recognisable again while the chicken kept hot in the oven. With a sigh of relief she unfastened her hair, shook it out vigorously, and sat down to attack her meal while she watched part of the inevitable TV soap on at this hour. Afterwards she drank some coffee and decided Charlie would be home by now. She ran downstairs and knocked on the door of the ground-floor flat. A girl with curly blonde hair and a beaming smile opened it, and Theo smiled back warmly.

'Hi, Nicola—your dear husband about? I have a bone to pick with him!'

Nicola Cowper pulled Theo inside, her pretty face rueful. 'I know, Theo—he told me. He was just about to run upstairs to grovel to you. Come and have a drink to make up. Charlie's such a wretch. Were you horribly embarrassed?'

'Of course she wasn't,' sang out a voice from the kitchen. 'Our Miss Grace lose her cool? Never!' Charlie came into the room with a bottle and some glasses, then clapped a hand to his eyes as he saw Theo. 'Only it's not Miss Grace, but our scrumptious Theodora restored to us once more.'

'A word in your shell-like ear, Charlie Cowper,' said Theo ominously, but accepted the glass of wine he proferred penitently. She cast a look at Nicola. 'Does your lady wife know the details?'

'You mean making passionate love to you on the

pavement in front of your boss?' Nicola nodded sympathetically. 'Charlie can be such a drongo on occasion.'

'But you love me really,' protested her husband.

'Can't think why!'

Charlie pulled his wife down on his knee and held his glass of wine to her lips. 'Seriously, though, Theo, I am sorry. Don't know what came over me. I suppose it was that prunes-and-prisms hairdo and those dire glasses. I couldn't resist the urge to steam them up. Did I cause trouble for you, love?'

'It all depends on what you mean by trouble.' Theo stared into her glass broodingly. 'It made my esteemed employer actually look at me for once. The fact that any man could actually bring himself to kiss me knocked him for six. Before today I was without even a gender as far as he was concerned. A sort of robot in skirts.'

'Is it any wonder!' Charlie shook his head in disapproval. 'Can't blame the chap if he only sees Miss Grace everyday. Why *do* you dress like that, Theo?'

She explained about the lovesick secretaries and her own bright idea of altering her appearance to get the job. 'All my fault,' she said ruefully. 'Years ago I read a Regency romance about a ravishing creature who makes herself look grotesque with wigs and false blemishes so the dashing marquis will engage her as governess to his wards.'

Charlie guffawed, almost unseating his wife, but Nicola nodded sagely as she looked from Theo's laughing eyes and mass of mahogany hair to the voluptuous curve of the breasts beneath the baggy sweater.

'Oh, I *see*,' she said, and smiled. 'So at last we know the reason for the double-act.'

'That's it, babies. And I'm sorry I ever started the

stupid charade! But now I'm stuck with it until I shake
the dust of Hackett Construction from my shoes,'
declared Theo, chuckling. 'Which may be a whole lot
sooner than I anticipated after your performance today,
Charlie Cowper.'

'Oh, rot!' said Charlie emphatically. 'Surely this
Hackett chap won't sling you out over a kiss!'

'No, no, I'm sure he won't. It's just that I don't relish
Hackett's new-found interest in my private life, that's
all.'

Nicola leaned forward, eyes shining. 'Did he take off
your glasses and find out how gorgeous you are without
them?'

'She will watch these old movies,' apologised Charlie,
and cast a curious look at Theo. 'What *was* the boss's
reaction once he found you were a person instead of a
machine?'

'He asked me my age—at least ten years less than he
thought from his surprise—and then told me I looked
ill.' Theo giggled at Nicola's disappointment and
finished her wine. 'Anyway, Charlie, my real reason for
coming down was to mention the revenge I took on you.'

'Tell me the worst?'

'Hackett asked me if I lived with you, so I said yes!'

Taking her leave of the laughing couple Theo ran
upstairs on winged feet, weariness forgotten in anticipation of the hours ahead with the other man in her life.
She locked the door of her room behind her, went over
to the desk at the window and switched on a goose-
necked lamp. Sitting down she opened a loose-leaf file
filled with narrow-ruled paper and began to read the last
twenty or so of the handwritten pages. She made a few
alterations, did a little ruthless cutting, then went on
with the next chapter of *The Fettered Heart*.

'Jason Harcourt,' she wrote rapidly, 'pushed the

goblet of wine across the table to the pale, defiant girl
standing before him. Her hair gleamed silver-gilt in the
flickering firelight, and he lounged back in his chair, his
ultramarine eyes travelling very slowly over her slender
shape, lingering longest where a jewel hung in the
shadowed hollow between her breasts.'

'How old are you?' he asked softly.

'Twenty, my lord.' Her low voice was icy with
contempt.

His eyes bored into hers. 'Does your confinement gall
you, my caged linnet? Dark shadows mar those
beautiful eyes. Are you ill?'

Theo scribbled on, transported at once to the cold
stone walls of a tower room in a castle where the man
who monopolised her leisure hours toyed delicately with
his beautiful, rebellious captive. Jason Harcourt, the
black-haired, blue-eyed hero of her novel, bore a
decided resemblance to James Hackett in looks and
ruthlessness, but in other ways he was light-years away
from her employer in charm, subtlety and utter
magnetism, as he kept the Lady Isabel hostage in
revenge on her brother, and gradually transformed his
captive's hatred of him into unwilling love that racked
her loyal soul with guilt.

CHAPTER TWO

NEXT morning Theo was more exhausted than ever. She had fully intended to stop writing before midnight but, as usual, it was two in the morning before she surfaced from her scribbling, with the result that she felt half dead as she left Willow Lodge for the short walk to Turnham Green next day. There was no Charlie Cowper this morning, for which she was grateful. She felt too tired to talk. The traffic seemed denser and noisier than ever to her ragged nerves, which were raw from lack of sleep and the black coffee gulped down to bring her back to life. As she walked as briskly as she could through the early morning crowds her mind was fully occupied, as it was every day at this time, with the work she had done the night before on her novel.

Theo couldn't remember a time when she hadn't been able to read. Her mother, a voracious reader herself, had encouraged her small daughter to follow her lead, to read everything she could lay hands on, and Theo early became an *habituée* of libraries and second-hand book shops. No matter how late she got home, or how strenuous her social life, she could never sleep at night without reading for a while before turning out her light. She read on the Underground, while she ate, in the bath, anywhere she could. To Theo reading was an addiction, but while Clare lived with her it had been kept in proportion. Together they had enjoyed a lively social life until Michael's advent, but once Clare became Mrs Blake and Theo was on her own, her old habits returned in full force, until one day, not long after starting her job

with Hackett Construction, she had been fired with the
idea of trying to write a book herself.

Historical backgrounds had always appealed to her
most, so she began by spending some time reading up on
the sixteenth century. Then she took James Hackett as
the physical model for her hero, dressed him in doublet
and hose, endowed him with all the virtues he appeared
to lack and added the vices she felt certain he did not,
and was ready to begin. Armed with a propelling pencil
and a lined block she launched herself into her first shot
at a historical novel with all the enthusiasm of a channel
swimmer headed for France.

At first she restricted the writing to weekends, and
kept up with some of the men she'd dated when she was
with the firm of insurance brokers in the City. But soon
the writing bug bit her hard. Her social life dwindled.
There were outcries from her parents when she
neglected to go home to Cheltenham for weeks at a time.
But until the book was finished Theo was determined to
keep her writing secret, cherishing it like a tender plant
that needed time to grow and become hardy before she
dared expose it to the cruel wind of criticism. Sometimes
she felt that her real life took place in her attic 'studio', as
Charlie grandly called it, that all her energy and
enthusiasm poured through her pencil on to the lined
pages. It was the other Theo, the tireless, self-effacing
Grace, who worked her efficient way through the day at
Hackett Construction, who was the unreal person—the
Theodora who took all the flak that James Hackett
dished out, soothed the ruffled feathers of his smarting
underlings, doled out aspirin for Hackett hangovers
with coffee from the expensive machine he had bought
for the purpose, and made convincing excuses to those
females importunate enough to defy the Hackett edict
and ring him at the office.

But the dual role was getting too strenuous, Theo knew only too well, unable to control a yawn as she reached the glass doors of the office building. To her amusement Anita, the receptionist, bade her good morning in unusually animated fashion, looking quite disappointed to see Mr Hackett's dowdy secretary alone and unembraced. Theo chuckled as she went up in the lift, but the smile was soon wiped from her face when she found her employer ransacking the filing cabinets in her office.

'Grace!' he roared, as he caught sight of her. 'You're late, and where the hell are all the Rocha do Sol files?'

'Good morning, Mr Hackett,' she said, unmoved, and took off her coat. 'I'm actually ten minutes early, and the Rocha do Sol records are, as usual, under R in the Algarve section of the cabinet devoted to Portugal.' She extracted the required documents and handed them to James Hackett before turning back to the cabinets to restore order from chaos. He lingered close by as she filed rapidly. Damn the man, she thought. Usually he stormed off without a word of thanks. And almost as though he could read her mind he said quietly, 'Thanks, Grace. I'm sorry.'

Sorry! From behind her large round lenses Theo stared at his tanned face in surprise. She gave a silent little nod of acknowledgement and went to sit at her desk to open the mail. To her intense irritation Hackett followed, and sat on the edge of it, watching her as she worked. He was dressed immaculately as usual, in one of his well-cut suits, dark blue this morning, with a white shirt and a plain silk tie a shade or two lighter than his suit, and the long foot he swung idly was shod in hand-sewn black calf of impeccable quality and gloss.

'You look even worse than yesterday, Grace,' he remarked.

Theo eyed him uneasily. What *was* he up to? she wondered. As a rule he would only have noticed any change for the worse in her if she had fallen unconscious at his feet. 'I'm perfectly well, Mr Hackett,' she assured him shortly.

'You look as though you could do with a good night's sleep,' he went on, a look in his eyes she didn't care for at all. 'That young man I saw you with yesterday—is he the cause of the circles under your eyes?'

Theo yearned to tell him to mind his own business, but contented herself with a curt negative in response.

'Then what *is* the matter, Grace?' The habitual note of command was missing for once from his voice. 'You're as pale as a ghost. Have you seen a doctor? You could be anaemic, or something. Perhaps you should take some iron pills. Don't get ill, for God's sake, you're the best secretary I've ever had, you know.'

Theo's eyes narrowed. Was he making fun of her? But James Hackett's handsome face was in deadly earnest and she swallowed in disbelief.

'I know I'm a bastard to work for, Grace,' he went on. 'Ben Arrowsmith was saying only yesterday what a miracle you are to put up with me.'

He was the one feeling ill, decided Theo. James Hackett was quite definitely not himself this morning. 'It's my job, Mr Hackett,' she said without emphasis, 'and it's very well paid.' She returned pointedly to her mail-sorting, and to her relief he finally took the hint and got to his feet, an unfamiliar look on his face as he stared down at her.

Then the telephone rang on Theo's desk, with someone demanding urgent conversation with the big white chief. In a flash Hackett reverted to his normal self as he strode into his office and began bellowing down the line the moment she put the call through.

The next few weeks wore on in much the usual way, apart from a definite change in James Hackett's manner towards her, as Theo grew daily more haggard and pallid. Each day was the normal series of crises strung on a chain of sheer hard work, while each evening she made her escape to another world of violence, intrigue and passion.

Spurred on by some inner compulsion that kept her writing into the small hours every day and most of the weekends, Theo at last threw down her pencil one Sunday evening in exhausted triumph. The book was finished. Done. She'd made it. Even if no one else ever read a word of it the book was completed, proof that she could maintain the self-discipline necessary to finish what she'd started. Theo felt like crowing with triumph, wishing there were someone to share the moment, but the only other people in the know were the publishers already in possession of the first three chapters. At the thought Theo sobered. What if they didn't like it, told her it was rubbish, that she had no talent? They had received her offering months ago. She was tired of waiting for it to turn up on the hall table with the post every morning, complete with rejection slip. Suddenly hungry, she made herself some supper, then cast a look at the remainder of the manuscript on the desk, three-quarters of it already typed. It was quite early. She could manage a couple of hours on the portable before bedtime easily.

Too easily. The couple of hours stretched to five before Theo was forced to call it a day, unable to decipher her own handwriting for the blurring of her tired eyes. She fell into bed, dead to the world and slept the heavy dreamless sleep of exhaustion all night, to wake next morning feeling remarkably fresh and invigorated, as though something wonderful had happened. A smile spread over her face as she lay looking at the sky through the small dormer window over her head. *The Fettered Heart* was finished at last, and the ravishing Isabel was safe in the arms of the irresistible Jason Harcourt, experiencing indescribable bliss at his strong, slender hands. Theo sighed. Lucky old Isabel.

Suddenly she stiffened. Admittedly it was June, but even so the sky looked very bright for this hour. She flew out of bed to the dressing table at the other end of the room where the raucous, two-legged alarm clock danced on a battered tin tray every morning to jolt her awake. In the annoying way of machinery, however, it needed a human hand to set the alarm, and last night, for the first time ever, she had forgotten. Small wonder she felt so chipper. It was past eleven. Theo moaned in horror and rushed to wash and dress, all fingers and thumbs as she hunted through drawers for underwear, and took a suit from her wardrobe. She was in her slip, her hair still all over the place as she tried to fasten a suspender, when a thunderous knocking made her jump yards.

'Yes?' she called. 'Who is it?'

'Hackett!' was the shattering answer. 'You're ill, aren't you? I *told* you to see a doctor. Why the hell didn't that man of yours ring up to tell us?'

Theo stood on one leg, transfixed, like a child playing Grandmother's Footsteps. Dear God, what on earth had possessed Hackett himself to come looking for her, she thought frantically, and snatched at her dressing-gown, hardly knowing which to cover up first, herself or her littered desk.

'Grace, let me in. If you're ill I'll get you to hospital,' bellowed the stentorian voice.

'Just a minute,' pleaded Theo, fervently hoping no one else was in the house by this time. She grabbed a bath towel from a drawer, veiled the desk and its contents with it and opened the door, pushing at her hair, forgetting too late that her glasses were on the dressing table.

James Hackett looked enormous on the narrow landing. Theo looked up at him, then back in despair at her narrow, unmade bed, and opened the door wider, motioning him to come in.

'Good morning,' she said, avoiding his eyes. 'Please come in. I'm terribly sorry to have put you to so much trouble, but I'm not ill, I just overslept—I forgot to set my alarm last night.'

The searching blue eyes tore themselves from their inspection of her face and person and gave a quick, comprehensive survey of the room. It was quite large, admittedly, but to the weakest of intellects it was glaringly obvious that she lived there alone. And, insensitive and overbearing though James Hackett might be, his intellect was no more puny than the rest of him. He closed the door behind him carefully, and looked her up and down, his blue eyes expressionless.

'I've had all the girls in the typing pool, plus what's-her-name who works for Ben Arrowsmith——'

'Carol Robson.'

'Yes, her. Everyone's been trying to find a phone number for you, but personnel could only come up with this address. How the devil does one get hold of you in an emergency?' he demanded.

'My family and close friends leave a message with the Cowpers who own the house, but they're both out during the day,' said Theo defensively, and looked pointedly at her watch.

'I had visions of your unconscious body on the floor, or something. You've never been late before.'

'And if possible I shan't be again,' she assured him tartly.

'Hm.' He stood just inside the door, rubbing his chin with one long finger. 'I didn't get in myself until half an hour ago, which is why no one realised you were missing. The Robson girl volunteered to come and see what was the matter, but I thought I'd better do it myself in case you needed hauling off to a casualty ward or whatever.'

'How very kind of you,' said Theo in a stifled voice. 'But if you'll leave me now I'll get dressed and be with you very shortly.'

Hackett didn't answer. He moved casually to the dressing table to examine the clock, then picked up the spectacles lying beside it and held them up to the light. 'Why do you wear these? They're plain glass.'

'Camouflage,' said Theo briefly, and looked with longing at the suit laid out on her bed, yearning for its protection. Her dressing-gown was perfectably respectable, but felt uncomfortably flimsy with her employer at such close quarters. Hackett followed her look with perfect comprehension, from the twitch at the corners of his mouth.

'You know, Grace,' he said conversationally, 'I would never have guessed how much hair you have, or how red it looks when its loose. Why do you screw it up to come to work?'

'Mr Hackett,' said Theo in desperation, 'please let me get dressed. If you'll just drive back to the office I'll follow as soon as I can, and stay later tonight to make up for the time lost.'

'I'll wait for you. The car's right outside.' There was mockery in his eyes as he shook his head reprovingly. 'You've been a right little deceiver, Miss Grace, haven't you, one way and another? You even told me you lived with the man I saw kissing you that time—yet this is a very chaste-looking apartment to me. Single bed, chintz skirt on the dressing table—all those books on the shelves. No girl with time to read that lot shares a room with a man.'

Theo ignored the last bit. 'Charlie Cowper does live in the same house, Mr Hackett. He's my landlord, and a compulsive practical joker. The kiss you witnessed was his idea of a fun way to start the day, I'm afraid.' Her patience was wearing thin. If only the man would leave so she could get dressed! Then she remembered something. The house had a main outer door kept permanently locked. 'How did you get in?' she asked, frowning.

'There was a cleaning woman in the hall.'

Theo's eyes closed momentarily. Now everyone in the house would know her boss had come rampaging after her. Mrs Campion dearly loved a good gossip.

'And after all that,' went on her relentless visitor, 'my errand of mercy was quite unnecessary. You aren't ill at all! In fact you look quite blooming this morning. If I'd met you in the street looking like that I'd never have recognised you.'

'Since I never go out in my dressing-gown that's highly unlikely,' she said acidly. 'Now, please, just give me a minute or two and I'll be with you.'

'Why on earth do you *do* it, Grace?' The gleam in his eye was unnerving.

'Do what?'

'Guy yourself up like your maiden aunt to come to the office.'

'I don't. My maiden aunt is thirty-seven, utterly gorgeous and a solicitor in Birmingham, Mr Hackett. The reason for the—the disguise is very simple really.' Theo gave him a terse account of Clare's information, and her own impulse to apply for the job looking as staid and colourless as she could since the salary was so tempting.

Hackett shook his head in wonder. 'Bloody good disguise it was, too. After the first week you just seemed to fade into the background, the archetypal perfect secretary. In fact, until I saw you being embraced with such enthusiasm I never thought of you in connection with the opposite sex at all.'

'Thank you,' she said sardonically.

'It isn't necessary, you know,' he assured her.

'What isn't necessary?'

'Making yourself look ugly to work for me. I've no objection to a good-looking secretary.' He grinned suddenly. 'On the contrary, I'm all for it since I happen to know this particular secretary can cope with my— er—bracing temperament, and is as efficient as hell.'

Theo regarded him thoughtfully, belatedly aware that it had been very good of him to come rushing to the bedside of his plain Jane of a secretary in what he assumed was her hour of need. 'Thank you for feeling concerned about me, anyway, Mr Hackett, it was very good of you. I can only apologise for wasting your time.'

'I don't consider it wasted at all. If I hadn't come barging in here this morning I might never have discovered the real Miss Grace.' He lifted a shoulder, looking suddenly rueful. 'I'm ashamed to say I have no idea what your first name is. Everyone seems to call you Grace.'

'Because you do.' Theo hesitated. 'Actually, it's Theodora. Theo for short.'

'I prefer Theodora,' he said, then turned brisk. 'Right. Leave Grace at home and I'll expect Theodora down in the car in——' he shot back a gleaming shirt cuff to consult the Rolex Oyster on his wrist. 'Fifteen minutes.'

'Ten will do.' Theo shut the door behind his large figure thankfully. Feeling all at sea, one way and another, she eyed her grey suit uncertainly, wondering what to wear. In the end she put it on, as planned, but with a pink silk shirt instead of her first choice of austere grey cotton. She brushed her hair and tied it at the nape of her neck with a black velvet ribbon, made up her face with its off-duty ration of blusher and eyeshadow, and indulged herself by wearing high-heeled grey patent leather pumps instead of her usual sensible black shoes. The hardest part was leaving off the spectacles. Without them she felt vulnerable as she ran downstairs to the gleaming Jaguar XJS standing outside Willow Lodge. James Hackett gave her an all-seeing inspection from the tips of her shoes to the crown of her shining head, and began to laugh quietly as she got in the passenger seat.

'The funny thing is,' he said at last, 'you don't really look all that different! And yet you're transformed. Amazing what glasses and a prim hairstyle can achieve as a disguise. As far as I can see your clothes look much the same as usual.'

'My leopard-skin body-stocking's at the laundry,' said Theo drily, but still he sat looking at her instead of switching on the ignition and getting them back to the office. She fidgeted in her seat, wondering what was on his mind.

'Theodora,' he said silkily, his eyes intent. 'A thought has just occurred to me. Now we know each other a little better are *you* likely to, well, nurture thoughts of a warmer nature, just like your predecessors?'

So that was it. Theo smiled coolly, shaking her head. 'No danger of that, Mr Hackett. You seem to be missing the point. You may feel you know *me* a little better, of course, but I already know *you* fairly well. Enough, anyway, to assure you with utmost sincerity that you can rest easy on *that* score. I have a man in my life who occupies my spare time very comprehensively.'

James Hackett looked irritatingly unconvinced. 'I'm not surprised. Someone must be the cause of the circles under your eyes. Nevertheless, I'm not sure your alleged immunity doesn't represent something of a challenge.'

'I do hope not, Mr Hackett.'

At the cold note of warning in Theo's voice the blue eyes narrowed. 'Why?' he asked sharply.

'Your views on keeping business and pleasure separate are well publicised.' She met his eyes levelly. 'It's a sentiment I share, Mr Hackett.'

'You mean it's all work and no play or—or what, precisely?'

'I hand in my notice.'

CHAPTER THREE

THEO'S revised appearance was something of a nine-day wonder in the company, and resulted in certain changes, some of them pleasant, others not. The other girls in the firm, most of whom had kept at a respectful distance previously, became more friendly. Carol Robson admitted frankly that 'Miss Grace' had frightened them all stiff, and asked slyly if Theo knew she was referred to as Amazing Grace behind her back. Theo laughed and told Carol she much preferred it to all the ribbing she was presently receiving from certain of the male members of staff. James Hackett had let them into the secret for Theo's disguise, and for a while she was teased unmercifully, but the novelty soon wore off. She was still 'Grace' to most people from force of habit, and since she had no intention of discarding the expensive tailored suits invested in for her role most of the employees at Hackett Construction quickly accepted the new-look Theo and in time forgot she had ever looked any different.

James Hackett was less adaptable. True he still called her 'Grace' in public, but in private kept to 'Theodora' with a deliberate whimsy that she disliked intensely. His whole attitude towards her was indefinably different from the impersonal air of the previous twelve months. Not that he made any attempt to treat her more gently or work her less hard. She still felt the lash of his irritation when the going was rough, but these days he had a habit of apologising for his outbursts afterwards, which underlined the change far more than the fact that she now felt free to wear a pretty dress on a sunny day, or make-up and perfume if she felt inclined, just like any other girl employed by his company—or anyone else's.

Eventually Theo finished typing her manuscript, tagged the pages together and put it away in her desk drawer before going home to Cheltenham for the weekend to tell her parents she was free of her Jekyll and Hyde existence since James Hackett's unexpected appearance on her doorstep that fateful morning. Hugh and Letty Grace were both very much amused, also keen to learn her employer's reaction. Mrs Grace was openly disappointed to find that life with the dynamic Mr Hackett was virtually unchanged, despite his discovery.

'I still wear the same clothes, you know, Mother,' said Theo, laughing. 'I haven't taken to appearing at the office in a taffeta ball-gown!'

Whatever she looked like, she was informed tartly, it was time her boss stopped working her so hard, and while she was home she could have a couple of early nights and eat some decent food. Theo agreed meekly, feeling slightly uncomfortable about misleading her parents as to the reason for her haggard apearance, and spent the entire weekend lying in the sun in the garden, or sleeping soundly in her familiar childhood bed. She returned to London late on the Sunday evening looking so much better that Charlie Cowper let out a loud wolf-whistle as he leaned out watering the geraniums in Nicola's window-boxes.

'You look rather more like the Theodora I first knew and lusted after,' he called, grinning. 'What kind of weekend have you had—naughty one in Brighton?'

'Filial one in Cheltenham,' corrected Theo, laughing. 'I'm full of Mother's spectacular cooking and I've lazed about in the sun all the time.'

'Good stuff. Some mail came for you yesterday.

Nicola kept it for you. Come and have a drink.'

Theo enjoyed a chat and a glass of wine with the congenial young Cowpers, then went upstairs leafing through her mail. There were the usual circulars, a letter from Clare she saw, brightening, then her heart began to pound as she realised there was a tiny crown logo on the last long white envelope. Diadem Publishing had finally answered. And there were no bulky pages of manuscript in the envelope.

Theo unlocked her door with fingers that shook, and flopped down on her bed to tear open the envelope. Her eyes widened incredulously as she read the short letter inside over and over again, her excitement so intense she could hardly take it in that Diadem thought the opening chapters of *The Fettered Heart* showed promise, and would like to see the rest of the manuscript. Theo leapt to her feet and did a war dance round the room in triumph, and was half-way through the door to share her news with the Cowpers when prudence checked her and she drew back. Better to wait for Diadem's opinion of the finished article first.

Her secret acted on Theo like a shot of adrenalin, and she fairly waltzed to work the following morning. The sound of the traffic was like music, the sun was warm on her arms, and she almost jogged along Chiswick High Road in her enthusiasm. She arrived at her desk very early, and was able to make inroads on the report left over from Friday before the mail arrived. Carol Robson called in on her way to her own desk and had a chat about the weekend until Mr Arrowsmith arrived, but there was no sign of James Hackett.

Theo had finished off the report, sorted out the post and even drafted replies to some of it before the man himself put in an appearance. One look at the grim black-browed face was enough to make Theo sorry he had. Outlook for the day stormy, she thought, resigned, as she went into his office.

James Hackett was sitting with his head in his hands as Theo handed over the cup of coffee ready for him as always. He looked up at her with bloodshot, morose eyes and reluctantly scanned the list of messages she gave him. The telephone on her desk had been ringing incessantly for the past hour with people demanding words with the chief, all of them answered with discreet dishonesty.

'Did you say I hadn't turned up this morning?' he demanded.

'No. I informed everyone you were unavailable until later.'

'Much later—like next week! Hell, Theodora, my head's splitting.'

'Too much sun?' she asked politely, and took the empty cup.

'Don't be snide,' he growled. 'You know very well I'm suffering—badly—from a hangover. Any painkillers?'

'Of course. More coffee?'

'As much as you've got. And tell everybody I'm still unavailable. Until midday, at least.'

'Very well, Mr Hackett.' Theo hid a smile as she went back to her office. When she returned Hackett was lying back in his chair with his eyes closed. He looked ghastly. You really tied one on last night by the look of you, thought Theo without sympathy. Aloud she said quietly, 'Your pills, Mr Hackett, and a glass of water. Drink as much of it as you can before your coffee.'

He eyed her malevolently as he followed her instruction. 'We appear to have changed roles, Theodora. You were like one of the walking dead until recently. Now it's me. What did you do over the weekend to get such a bucolic glow, for God's sake?'

'I spent it with my parents. More coffee, Mr Hackett?' Theo looked on dispassionately as he stared into his cup, lips compressed. Then he swallowed hard and jumped to his feet abruptly, tearing from the room with a muttered curse. Theo took away the empty cup and glass, and when the sufferer returned, mopping his ashen face, she was installed in her usual chair in front of the desk, all the important mail of the day arranged neatly at his place, waiting for him. He sat down and stared at it without enthusiasm.

'I feel lousy,' he stated.

'Shall we leave it for a while, then, Mr Hackett? I have plenty to get on with.' Theo rose, checked by his mirthless chuckle.

'What a perfect secretary you are, Theodora,' he said wryly. 'What would I do without you?'

'No one's indispensable, Mr Hackett.'

'Some more than others, I suspect.' He eyed her gloomily. 'You make me feel worse just to look at you. Won the pools, or something?'

'I wish I had!'

He leaned his chin on one hand. 'And what would you do if you did? Resign from your job at once, I suppose.'

Theo nodded affably. 'Then buy a country cottage and a dog.' And write all day long in peace, she added privately as she closed the door quietly behind her.

It was only a short time before James Hackett felt restored enough to take up the reins, and Monday proceeded as usual. Theo was obliged to refuse lunch with Carol, and only took enough time off to nip out to post her manuscript before hurrying back through tempting sunshine to the report that had to be ready for a meeting later in the afternoon. Just before the meeting was due to begin Hackett strode into her office.

'Look, Theodora,' he said, sighing, 'it's entirely my

fault, I know, but at the moment I can't see light at the end of the tunnel. Would it throw your arrangements out for this evening to stay on for an hour to clear up some of the chaos on my desk?'

Theo was surprised. It was nothing new for her to work late when the occasion demanded it, but this was the first time she had been requested to do so in such conciliatory terms. Poor old Grace would have been taken for granted, but the more personable Theodora rated smoother handling, it seemed.

'Not in the least,' she said crisply. 'The report on the sports complex is ready, Mr Hackett. Copies are laid out on the boardroom table. José Morais rang from Rocha do Sol while you were out, but will ring back at six.'

The hour James Hackett had requested ran on into more than two by the time the backlog of work was cleared, and Theo's earlier glow had diminished by the time he called it a day. As she was leaving he caught up with her at the lift.

'I'll drive you home,' he offered as they descended.

'No, really. I'd rather walk. Since it's such a lovely evening I'll be glad of the fresh air. But thank you for the thought,' she added.

Hackett leaned an arm above her and stared down into her face irritably. 'You puzzle me, Theodora.'

'Probably because you have two names for me these days,' she said calmly. 'If you stuck to Grace it would be simpler, Mr Hackett.'

'My friends call me Jem,' he said unexpectedly, as the lift reached the ground floor. Theo disliked the suggestion, if that was what it was. He might be the jewel in the crown to his girlfriends, but he was not going to be Jem to his secretary.

'Really?' she parried, and preceded him into the evening sunshine.

'Couldn't you do the same?'

'You can't be serious, Mr Hackett!'

He shrugged his powerful shoulders. 'I suppose not. The rest of the staff would think the worst, now you've come out of your chrysalis. Pity.' He smiled suddenly. 'Pity about this man in your life too. If it weren't for him we could go out of town and have dinner somewhere on the river as a token of appreciation for your working so late.'

'No, thank you. I'll just put in for overtime as usual, Mr Hackett.' Theo smiled back to take the edge off her words. 'Attractive though the offer is.'

'If this man wasn't in the background—would you come?'

'To be frank—no. As I said before, I believe business and pleasure should be kept separate.'

A rather smug smile curled James Hackett's wide, well-cut mouth. 'Then it would have been a pleasure, I take it?'

'Of course. Dinner on the river on an evening like this? Bliss! Goodnight, Mr Hackett.' Theo smiled pleasantly and walked away, fairly certain James Hackett was watching her out of sight. She frowned a little, not at all sure she cared for the interest he was showing signs of taking in her. She was the same person inside that she had been all along. It was only the packaging that was different. But Hackett was the sort of man who appreciated packaging. The only reason he would have to remove it would be to gain access to the body inside, she felt sure, with no regard for the mind inside *that*.

Over a solitary salad later Theo felt a fleeting regret for the dinner she could have eaten beside the river, wherever that might have been. Of course, if she stood on a chair and craned her neck she could see the Thames from her own room, so in one way James Hackett had been offering nothing new to her. She chuckled at the thought, then forgot him as she began thinking about her book, and wondering how long it would be before she heard again from Diadem. It would be harder to be patient this time, now the carrot of hope was dangling in front of her nose. Before, she had been aiming into the unknown, but this time she had the doubtful encouragement of knowing her writing had 'promise'. Theo would have given much to tell someone about it, but she resisted the temptation to ring home or rush down to Charlie and Nicola, and went to bed with her latest haul from the second-hand book shop she haunted in her lunch hours.

As the summer wore on Theo grew restless, and began reading up on the Crusades in her spare time, which hung heavy now that her novel was finished. Between herself and her employer a new kind of working relationship had been established. Still abrasive, James Hackett was nevertheless more friendly and a lot easier to work for these days, and never overstepped the line Theo made clear she felt existed between them. He took pleasure instead in giving her extra little chores like sending flowers to his latest conquest, or choosing gifts for him to donate in apology for the times he broke appointments when some crisis arose on one of his various UK building sites. Theo enjoyed his absences, utilising them to catch up on routine, and indulge in the luxury of a longer lunch break. During one of the latter she ran into one of her former escorts, and began to meet him again occasionally for dinner or the theatre, and made a point of going home to Cheltenham more regularly for weekends.

Then one day towards the end of July, Theo ran downstairs to find a letter from Diadem on the hall table.

It was from one Miles Hay, editorial director of their fiction department, telling her he considered her novel worth publishing. A few minor adjustments and cuts were necessary, he wrote, but otherwise he felt it had every chance of success, and would Miss Grace find it convenient to lunch with him on Friday of the following week. Would she! Theo clasped the letter to her in triumph. The Cowpers, unfortunately, had already left for the day, so she was obliged to walk to Turnham Green with her glorious news ticking inside her like a time bomb.

She decided against telling anyone at the office about her book, mainly because she shuddered at the thought of Hackett's learning about it, convinced his reaction would be scathing if he discovered she had written a romantic novel. Romance was not something she associated with James Hackett. And Friday as a day off was hardly likely to meet with his approval, either. It would be necessary to phrase her request with the utmost care, and to wait for a propitious moment.

The latter seemed unlikely to occur for some little while, she discovered when she arrived. James Hackett was already at his desk, conducting a heated exchange with someone at the other end of the telephone in Portugal. Theo waited until all was quiet before she took in the post and bade him a quiet good morning.

The hard blue eyes gazed absently at her as he answered, 'There's a hold-up with the opening at Rocha do Sol, would you believe. I was all set to go there this weekend, and now it's been put forward a week. Get a plane reservation with TAP for next week, would you— or make it two. You'd better come along as well.'

Theo's eyes opened wide. 'To Portugal, Mr Hackett?'

'That's where the Algarve was last time I was there! I'll need a report on the complex, so the quickest way is to take you with me. Anyway,' he added, 'I could do with some sort of hostess at the opening.'

'Some sort of hostess'! Hackett's turn of phrase held a definite lack of charm on occasion for Theo. Suddenly she went cold.

'When would you want to go, Mr Hackett?'

'Fly out Thursday, the opening's on Friday, fly back Saturday.'

'And it's next week.'

'Something wrong with next week?'

Theo braced herself. 'I was hoping for that particular Friday off.'

'Can't be done,' he said flatly. 'Postpone whatever it is and take the day off some other time. Two days, if you want.'

It could be her wedding day for all he cared, thought Theo bitterly, and tried one last appeal. 'It really is very important to me, Mr Hackett.'

'And the Rocha do Sol opening is very important to me! For God's sake, stop being so awkward and ring up this man of yours and explain.' He waved irritably towards the telephone. 'I presume he's the cause of all the panic?'

Without a word Theo turned on her heel and went back to her own office to ring Diadem. Miles Hay was out, his secretary informed her, and suggested Friday of the following week for the postponed lunch date, promising to write confirming it.

'All fixed?' asked Hackett later from the doorway.

Theo nodded stonily and turned her attention to the post, too incensed to say anything more as she began working at a furious speed, her lips tightly compressed.

'You look like the Grace of old with that expression on your face,' James Hackett informed her. 'Will the trip to

Rocha do Sol mess up your social life so very badly, then?'

Theo turned hostile eyes up to his and shook her head. 'I needed the day off for a business appointment, not a social occasion, Mr Hackett.'

He moved towards her, his face like thunder. 'An interview for another job?'

Theo was sorely tempted to say yes, but truth prevailed. 'No, nothing like that.'

He waited, obviously expecting her to enlarge, but when she said no more he shrugged and told her to get a move on with the post, as he had a full day ahead of him. Theo did as she was bidden, but her feelings of resentment ran high all day. The irony of the trip to Portugal was that at any other time the prospect would have delighted her. She had spent a holiday in the Algarve with Clare once, and loved it. But even the charms of that beautiful coast paled in comparison with an interview with a publishing house. Trips to various sites with James Hackett were quite customary but only for a day within the UK, and always in the company of one or two other men from the firm. The Algarve was a new departure. The project there was Hackett's major concern at the moment, she knew, but Theo was annoyed with fate for timing the opening to coincide with her own appointment with Miles Hay.

It was fairly late in the afternoon, while Hackett was in the throes of a very heated meeting with his finance director, that Theo answered the telephone to a lady with a familiar, husky voice, who insisted on talking to 'Jem' no matter how busy he was, assuring Theo that he wouldn't mind once he knew who wanted him. Theo doubted it strongly, but pressed the necessary button and when Hackett's 'Yes?' barked at her, informed him there was an urgent call for him and put it through. She put down her receiver with a smile of pure malice, some of her resentment cooling a little, soothed at the thought of her employer's fury over the interruption.

Theo was about to leave when the noisy discussion in the other office finally ended, and James Hackett strode towards her, his face dark with fury.

'You knew bloody well I was having problems with Barrett in there! Why the hell did you put that call through to me in the middle of it?' he demanded.

Theo picked up her bag, unmoved. 'According to the lady it was a matter of life and death, so I felt you should decide whether she was right, not me.'

'A matter of life and death to Chloë Masson is some party tonight. I felt a right berk putting her off with Barrett listening in, I can tell you. Dammit, Grace, I pay you to cope with exigencies like that.'

'I'm sorry,' said Theo untruthfully. 'If you're dissatisfied with my work, of course, I'll resign.'

James Hackett stopped short, glaring at her in frustration. 'For God's sake stop giving me your resignation every five minutes. Can't I offer a little criticism these days?'

'You were shouting at me at the top of your voice,' she pointed out.

'Was I?' He sighed heavily. 'It's been one of those days, I suppose.'

Not for me, thought Theo happily, all her resentment gone now, as she hugged her secret to herself. 'It usually is,' she said drily.

'You never answered me back once upon a time.'

'The type of female I was pretending to be would have been incapable of it. I'm afraid the real me isn't nearly as docile.' Her eyes met his candidly, and James Hackett's narrowed to a hard blue gleam.

'I've noticed that for some time. You don't really like

me very much, do you, Theodora?'

'As I keep reminding you, Mr Hackett, I don't allow personal feelings to enter into it when it comes to my job.'

'Or you'd have walked out on me long ago, I suppose.' His wrath had cooled into wry amusement by this time, and a smile twitched the corners of his mouth as he sat on the edge of her immaculately tidy desk. 'Go on, Theodora. Tell the truth.'

'There have been times when I've been tempted,' she admitted.

'So what made you stay?'

'The money, Mr Hackett. You pay me very well.'

'What do you spend it on?' he asked curiously. 'A car? Social life?'

'I don't drive, and I don't go out all that much,' said Theo with candour. 'Since I don't share it my flat is a bit expensive, but my real extravagance is books.'

He nodded. 'I remember. Your room had more books than furniture.' From the look on his face it was evident he was also remembering the Theo of that morning. 'That's the only time I've seen you flustered, Theodora, come to think of it.'

'With reason,' she said colourlessly. 'I must go now ——Oh, but while I think of it, should I be seeing to all the Algarve arrangements?'

'Only the airline tickets. José Morais will see to things the other end.' He got up to open the door for her. 'And bring a bikini. As you've seen from the model, there'll be a pool at your disposal.'

Theo looked at him questioningly. 'Just *two* tickets, Mr Hackett?'

'That's right, Theodora.' He grinned down at her lazily. 'Just you and me.'

As Theo walked home she thought of the last words

with misgiving, not caring much for the gleam in James Hackett's eyes as he'd said them. The early sunshine had given way to grey drizzle and she began to hurry back to Willow Lodge, happy to meet Nicola Cowper as she ran up the steps to the house. At last there was someone to hear her wonderful news and Nicola's crow of excitement could be heard all over the house as she insisted on Theo coming into the ground floor flat to ring her parents in Cheltenham.

'Why didn't you tell us before?' demanded Letty Grace, when the excitement died down a little.

'Had to see if I was any good first—and it actually seems as if I may be. Isn't it amazing?'

'Not amazing at all, darling. I can't wait to read it!'

'I haven't even had the interview with Diadem yet,' laughed Theo, and explained about the Algarve trip and Hackett's refusal to give her the day off.

'Leave!' said Mrs Grace trenchantly.

'Not yet. But soon perhaps.'

When Charlie arrived he swept both girls into a communal embrace when he heard the news, kissing them both impartially, then he released Theo to eye her accusingly. 'Why weren't we in the know, then?'

Theo smiled sheepishly. 'Oh, you know how it is, Charlie. Most people think they could write a book if they only had the time, so I wanted my effort accepted before sounding off about it. And even if it is published I'll never win the Booker McConnell prize, or anything,' she added. 'It's what's known as a "bodice-ripper", Charlie, all heaving bosoms and passion and swordplay, and all that.'

'Scrumptious,' said Nicola, and smiled knowingly. 'So now we know what you've been doing with yourself lately! Charlie and I thought it rather odd that you never seemed to go out anywhere at night.'

Theo grinned happily. 'I've been spending my nights with Sir Jason Harcourt, of the raven hair and blue, blue eyes, and charm enough for ten!'

The three of them went out for a Chinese meal to celebrate and enjoyed a happy, noisy evening together, sitting over a couple of bottles of wine afterwards at Willow Lodge until well into the small hours, drinking success to Theo's novel and confusion to Theo's boss, the villain of the piece, considered pretty low by Charlie and Nicola to refuse the necessary time off for the all-important interview. Theo felt obliged to point out that Hackett had no idea why she wanted that particular day off, also that the alternative was a trip to Portugal, not something to be sneezed at in the ordinary way of things.

'Mrs Campion told me he's rather tasty, if he's the one who came looking for you one morning,' commented Nicola.

'Yes, I suppose he is, if you like them big and dark. Socially he's a wow with the girls. But yours truly sees the other side of the coin most of the time, unfortunately.'

'Well, speaking personally, I'm grateful to him for barging in here like that. At least it's put paid to Miss Prunes and Prisms.' Charlie leered evilly at Theo. 'When he burst into your room I trust you were fully dressed, Miss Grace?'

'More or less. But my cover was blown at first glance. Not that I'm sorry, since the real me wasn't fired on the spot—probably because I'd survived a whole year beforehand without succumbing to the so-called Hackett charm.'

Due to far too much wine and too little sleep Theo looked a bit wan next morning. She brightened when she found a letter from Diadem confirming the postponed meeting with Miles Hay, but her early morning walk to

Turnham Green did nothing for her thumping head-ache and she had a disinclination for company of any kind, let alone that of James Hackett, who was prowling up and down in her small office when she arrived.

'Good morning,' he said brusquely. 'Let's make a start right away, please. I'd like to be on my way to Birmingham within the hour.'

Theo yearned for coffee, but the prospect of a Hackett-free day cheered her up while she sat doggedly making notes of all his instructions, her pencil flying over the pages of her notebook.

'Right. Coffee,' said James Hackett at last, and Theo hurried off to make it, deeply thankful. While the coffee was perking she fetched herself a glass of water and swallowed two of the painkillers kept for managerial hangovers and looked up to find her employer watching her sardonically from the doorway.

'You should tell him to go home earlier, Grace,' he said.

Theo bit back the retort she would have liked to make, and poured two cups of coffee, handing one in silence to the man scrutinising her pale face with interest.

'The dark circles under your eyes are back,' he remarked.

'A slight headache, nothing that will keep me from my work,' Theo informed him shortly.

'That wasn't what I meant,' he said irritably. 'You look ill, that's all.'

'I'm not ill, Mr Hackett, thank you. I drank more wine than usual last night and went to bed much too late.'

'Celebrating something?' His tone was sharp. 'Not getting engaged, or anything, were you?'

'No, Mr Hackett.' Theo's polite finality sent James

Hackett back into his office, a scowl on his handsome face.

'I'll be back tomorrow,' he informed her later, as he left. 'I'm sure you'll cope with all eventualities in my no doubt welcome absence.'

'I'll do my best,' she assured him serenely.

James Hackett loomed very large in the doorway as he leaned there for a moment, looking her very deliberately in the eye when she glanced up in enquiry.

'Of that, Theodora, I never have the slightest doubt,' he drawled softly, and went off before she could think of a reply.

CHAPTER FOUR

ONCE her appointment with Miles Hay was confirmed Theo firmly put thoughts of her novel from her mind and began to look forward to the trip to Rocha do Sol. Secretly she was rather pleased at the prospect of a day or two in the sun, particularly since the British summer was playing very hard to get.

'I envy you,' sighed Carol Robson, as she watched rain sluicing down the window. 'I only wish Mr Arrowsmith was needed there as well, and me with him.'

'I suppose I'd better buy something to wear,' said Theo, without much enthusiasm. 'Mr Hackett mentioned some sort of reception, and I don't have anything very fancy in my wardrobe these days. Any spare cash has gone on tailored stuff since I came to work here.'

Carol laughed. 'Then now's your chance to lash out on something spectacular. *I* would. In fact I'd sell my soul for a weekend in the sun with your boss, believe me!'

Not at one with Carol on that point, Theo nevertheless spent the following Saturday in Cheltenham with her mother in search of 'something pretty' as the latter put it.

'When Edwina was here last weekend she found a quite lovely dress to wear to some legal dinner,' said Mrs Grace.

'How *is* my maiden aunt?'

'Rushing about like a human dynamo as usual—and for heaven's sake never let her hear you call her that!'

'How's her weekend retreat coming along?' Theo asked.

'The cottage is more or less finished, I believe. Edwina's very pleased with it, and with the location. You know how fond she is of that area around Chipping Campden. She says you're to visit her there once the furniture is in.'

'Good. I'll take her up on it. Now where exactly did she run this gorgeous creation to earth, Mother dear?'

Theo was as successful as Edwina had been, but paid rather more than she had intended for a ravishingly simple dress of a subtle dull pink, with a sheen to its silk texture that accentuated the red lights in her hair and gave her skin added glow.

'Very nice indeed,' approved Mrs Grace, then frowned. 'I hope your Mr Hackett isn't susceptible to bare shoulders, Theo.'

'Not my shoulders, Mother. And even if he is, my views on keeping business and pleasure separate are well known to him, don't worry!'

Mrs Grace looked unconvinced, then insisted on paying for a pair of fragile sandals to match the dress. 'Pity to spoil the ship!' she said cheerfully.

James Hackett drove Theo to Heathrow the following Thursday through pouring rain. 'Ever been to the Algarve?' he asked.

'Yes, once. I went to Albufeira with a friend a couple of years ago and enjoyed it enormously. I loved the Portuguese, they're such charming, friendly people.'

'Good. You'll be meeting a lot of them at the opening tomorrow night.' He gave her a quick look. 'No problem about leaving your man on his own this weekend?'

'No,' said Theo shortly. 'None.'

He took the hint and abandoned personal matters, appearing to take pains to be attentive and courteous.

Throughout the flight he took care of Theo with a solicitude that disarmed and surprised her. It was small wonder his girlfriends were thick on the ground, she reflected, or that there was such wailing and gnashing of teeth when he deserted them for pastures new. Theo settled down to enjoy the trip, and even took a detached pleasure in travelling with such an attractive escort. Approve of him or not, there was no denying that James Hackett was far and away the most handsome companion she'd ever had, and for the time being a very different cup of tea from the tyrant who held Hackett Construction on such a tight rein.

The site manager of Rocha do Sol, José Morais, met them at Faro airport. He was a short, slim man with twinkling dark eyes, but his thin, clever face went blank with surprise as he was introduced to Theo.

'*Muito prazer*, Miss Grace, I am so happy to meet the owner of the charming voice on the telephone,' he said, and shot a questioning glance at Hackett. 'I did not realise Miss Grace was coming, James.'

'Thought she'd come in useful,' said Hackett blandly, and ushered Theo into the car.

The models of Rocha do Sol had been familiar to Theo since her start at Hackett Construction and she could have sketched the site accurately from memory, but nothing had prepared her for the brilliant beauty of the clifftop reality when they arrived there. In the golden sunshine the houses were blindingly white against the green of new lawns, softened already here and there by the whites and pinks of bush geranium and mesembryanthemums despite the newness of the development.

When the car drew up outside the red-roofed, glass-walled restaurant and club which dominated the site, James Hackett was out of it in a flash and immediately on his way to inspect everything, signalling Theo to follow him. José Morais led the way to the newly completed pool framed in greenery, the well-patronised tennis courts, the small palm-thatched bar nearby, the solarium, and the steps leading down through the golden rocks to the sand and sea below.

Many of the houses were already occupied by permanent residents, José explained to Theo, those nearest the clubhouse reserved for holiday lets. All the main construction work was complete, but some of the houses lacked fittings and landscaping work on the gardens, he said in response to James Hackett's quick-fire catechism, but everything was in hand for the opening the following day. Theo followed behind as her employer inspected everything, his lynx-keen eyes everywhere as he pointed out areas where improvements could be made. Only the last few houses nearest the cliff edge were unoccupied, and the overall effect of the entire place was one of great beauty, constructed with taste and sympathy to blend with the surrounding landscape.

'Not bad, José,' was the verdict, as James Hackett finally turned back. 'You've made good progress since my last visit. Where have you put us, by the way?'

The man gave Theo an unhappy glance. 'A slight difficulty, James. I did not realise—I mean, if I had known I would have kept two of the single rooms free at the club.'

Hackett shrugged indifferently. 'Anywhere will do, José—it's only for a night or two.'

Theo stiffened as she found she was expected to share one of the most recently completed houses with her boss. With a worried frown José expressed the hope that Miss Grace would have no objection since the house was large, with several rooms, and some way from the occupied houses, and therefore quite private.

James Hackett met the suspicion in Theo's eyes blandly, then smiled at the site manager. 'I don't mind, José.'

José spread his hands in apology, obviously aware of Theo's lack of enthusiasm. 'Perhaps I could move one of the guests——'

'No,' said Hackett instantly. 'We're in business to attract guests and holidaymakers, not inconvenience them. I'm sure we'll manage, won't we, Grace?'

Theo looked at him in eloquent silence, then relented at the sight of José Morais' obvious distress. 'Please don't worry, Mr Morais. As Mr Hackett says, it's only for a short time.'

Nevertheless, when they were alone at the Villa Farol Theo found it difficult to hide her displeasure when Hackett picked up her luggage and asked her which bedroom she fancied. Theo inspected the rooms in hostile silence. There were three to choose from, two of them furnished, separated by one that still lacked a bed. Theo chose the smallest room nearest the kitchen. 'There was no mention of sharing accommodation,' she said coldly.

Hackett shrugged. 'Originally I intended bringing Chloë, but I forgot to mention the change of plan to José. Don't blame him, please. The fault is mine.'

'I'm sure it is, Mr Hackett.' Theo felt tired and grubby and very cross. 'Yet you must have known how I'd feel about it!'

He leaned in the doorway, arms folded. 'Now steady on, Theodora. Granted you look a bit different these days, but don't imagine I have any ideas about falling on you with ravening lust just because you don't hide behind those ridiculous spectacles any more.' He pushed himself away from the door and gave her an unamused, mocking smile. 'Since your privacy's so precious to you

I'll take myself off for an hour to meet the rest of the staff. I'll be back about nine to shower before dinner at the club restaurant. Be ready.'

Alone, Theo fumed, but a long soak in her own private bathroom went a long way to smoothing her ruffled feathers, and afterwards, in a cool dress of white-dotted terracotta voile, she explored the house alone while she had the opportunity. It smelled very new, but the lingering traces of paint in the air took nothing from the charm of the one-storey building, which was circular, like the lighthouse on the nearby promontory that gave the house its name. Curving olive-green couches followed the line of the walls in the living-room, either side of a stone fireplace with a deep, white-cowled Algarve chimney-piece. Several small tables held copper lamps with amber shades near deep armchairs, and through an arch Theo found a dining area with heavy carved furniture and shelves against stark white walls where colourful plates of local pottery provided a necessary note of contrast.

She had a look in the small, well-equipped kitchen, and made herself a cup of coffee, wandering out with it through the glass doors of the living-room to linger on the patio, listening to the sound of the sea far below as she admired the stars reflected in the swimming pool. Impressed with the house, and the whole of Rocha do Sol, Theo made a wry face as she remembered the cost of owning a house like this, then smiled. Perhaps one day she might write a best-seller and be able to afford a life in the sun.

Her pleasant musings were interrupted by the sound of footsteps on the patio, which encircled the entire house. James Hackett came into view, his face dark against the white of his shirt, his jacket slung over his shoulder.

'Reconciled now to the accommodation?' he demanded.

'Yes, Mr Hackett.'

'Good. I'll be with you in fifteen minutes.'

In slightly shorter time than promised he rejoined Theo, newly shaved and his hair still damp. 'I had a couple of drinks with José and his crew,' he said, and led the way indoors to the living-room, which was softened now by an amber glow from the lamps. 'What will you have?'

'Wine, possibly?'

'In Portugal? What better?' He went to the kitchen and returned with a bottle of chilled white Palmela, then poured a glass for Theo. She sat down on one of the couches, and her companion leaned against the chimney-piece. Tonight, she noted with detachment, James Hackett looked even more attractive than usual in an informal combination of fawn trousers with an unlined cream linen jacket and a white shirt open at the throat. And for once his eyes were neither hard nor mocking as they regarded her steadily.

'I *am* sorry—truthfully, Theodora. I plain forgot to tell José about the change of plan.' He looked down into his glass, frowning a little. 'And my remarks about your physical assets were uncalled for. Glasses or no glasses, you're a very attractive lady, and how the hell I never noticed it sooner is something I can't fathom out.'

Somewhat mollified, Theo smiled. 'You saw me as I meant you to see me. I set out to be the kind of woman I heard you wanted for the job and you took me at face value.'

His eyes moved over her dispassionately, lingering longest at the neckline of her dress. 'I must have been blind. If I'd ever given it a thought I'd have sworn 'Miss Grace' had as much shape as an ironing board, yet—at the risk of offending you—these days it's obvious to anyone with half an eye that your shape is the sort other women envy. How the blazes did you *do* it?'

Theo coloured a little, and sipped her wine. 'Suits with matching waistcoats, occasionally a tailored dress a size too big when the weather was warm.' She looked up at him in challenge. 'It was easy, because you never actually looked at me, anyway.'

He shook his head in wonder. 'As I said, blind as a bat.'

'Not entirely. You noticed I was looking tired, eventually.'

'Only after most of my colleagues commented on the fact.' He grinned. 'It put the wind up me, I can tell you.'

'Afraid you'd be put to the trouble of finding a replacement if I actually expired at your feet?' suggested Theo slyly.

'Something like that.' James Hackett smiled impenitently and held out his hand. 'Come on, let's eat. I'm starving.'

They were given a table near the glass wall of the crowded restaurant, and presented with a superbly cooked meal. Theo, indulging her passion for fish, ate her way through king-sized prawns and a lobster salad with relish, watched with amusement by her companion as he kept her glass filled with local wines bearing exotic, unpronounceable names.

'It's a change to watch a woman enjoying her dinner,' he commented. 'Nothing so depressing as a companion who picks at lettuce leaves and drinks mineral water.'

From which Theo deduced his latest lady was on a diet, and smiled ruefully at the thought of the thickly buttered bread consumed with her meal, not to mention the cream-drenched slice of gâteau the waiter was setting in front of her at that very moment.

'And yet I read somewhere that to a man a hearty appetite on a woman is about as alluring as football boots, Mr Hackett,' she remarked.

'Can't you bring yourself to call me by my first name?' he said swiftly, and, to her surprise, after the wonderful food and potent wine, Theo found she could quite easily.

'All right. James, then,' she conceded.

'Not Jem?'

Theo remembered the throaty voice on the telephone and shook her head. 'No. I don't think so. I'll stick to James—*pro tem.*'

He laughed, and asked permission to smoke a cigar when coffee was served. Theo nodded, fixing him with a bright, enquiring look.

'Why *did* you bring me here instead of Chloë—Miss Masson, I mean—as originally planned?'

James leaned back lazily in his chair, his eyes narrowed through the blue smoke. 'For one thing I genuinely do need you to record tomorrow's meeting, and for another, as from a week or so back Chloë Masson and I are no longer—friends.'

'I'm sorry,' said Theo quickly.

'Don't be. It was never more than a passing fancy.'

'Yours or hers?' she heard herself saying.

He laughed softly. 'Whichever way I answer that will sound wrong, so let's say I suggested to Chloë that we settle for friendship.'

'But she disagreed.'

'Exactly. Chloë had her sights set on matrimony.'

'Ah!'

'And my views on matrimony are well known to you, I imagine.' He gave her a searching look. 'And what about you, Theodora? Do you intend marrying this man of yours?'

Theo stared at him blankly for a moment, then recalled herself hurriedly. 'Oh—Jason,' she said unguardedly. 'No. I'm afraid marriage just isn't possible.'

James leaned across the table, his brows drawn together. 'You mean the guy's *married*?'

Theo swallowed hard and nodded, her eyes dropping at the sudden blaze in the blue ones holding hers.

'What the hell are you doing wasting yourself on a married man?' he demanded. 'Or is he getting a divorce so he can marry you?'

'No. He—he can't.'

'Religious reasons, I suppose?'

'Could we change the subject, please?' Theo cast an eye about her in desperation. 'Will the reception be held here tomorrow night?'

Reluctantly James subsided, frowning, but followed her lead. 'Yes. Drinks, buffet dinner. I hope you brought your party dress.'

'Of course. But I thought my notebook and pencil were more important from your point of view!'

'Not a bit of it. I'd like you to look on this trip as a little break.' He smiled at her ruefully. 'God knows, you deserve one just for putting up with me.'

Theo could hardly believe her ears, and looked up at him in suspicion as he came to hold her chair for her. 'You're uncharacteristically mellow tonight,' she said candidly, as they left the restuarant.

James shrugged as they strolled along. 'I am what I am by my own efforts, Theodora Grace, and I haven't got to the top of my own particular little tree by being soft-centred. My father was a small provincial builder who went bankrupt, and my mother comes from Welsh coal-mining stock. I am, as the saying goes, a self-made man—not a breed noted for being mellow!'

Lamps in wrought-iron holders cast golden pools of

light in the scented darkness, and as they passed one Theo examined the hard, predatory profile of her companion closely. 'Are your parents dead?'

'My father died years ago, but my mother is very much alive.' He chuckled. 'She'd like you, Theodora. Your ruse of disguising yourself to get the job would amuse her no end.'

'It amused my own parents at first, but as time went on they grew worried. Neither of them have much time for anything even remotely dishonest.'

They reached the Villa Farol and James unlocked the heavy carved door and went in ahead of Theo, switching on lights. He turned to look at Theo questioningly. 'How did *you* feel about it?'

'It was a terrible drag having to make myself as hideous as possible every day, but otherwise I felt perfectly justified. I wasn't doing anything wrong.' She smiled at him serenely. 'I earned my money every day and still do, so from my point of view I wasn't breaking any rules. You wanted a non-nubile, super-efficient robot. I wanted the salary you were offering, so it seemed like fair exchange.'

The gleaming blue eyes scrutinised her slowly from top to toe. 'No one can say you look non-nubile these days!'

Theo's smile grew mocking. 'Ah, but nubile means marriageable, Mr—James. Marriage doesn't figure in my plans at all, I assure you.'

James stood looking down at her from his formidable height, his long fingers stroking his chin. 'There are less formal arrangements than marriage, Theodora.'

'A lover, you mean?' She nodded soberly. 'I know—I already have one, as I told you earlier. Thank you for dinner. Goodnight.'

'Goodnight, Theodora.' There was something unsettling about his tone, and the smile that accompanied it, and Theo left the big room quickly, suddenly needing the safety of her own bedroom. With its door safely bolted behind her she opened the window and let in the sea-scented air, then prepared rapidly for bed, more than a little weary after a day spent in James Hackett's bracing company. James. It seemed strange to think of him like that. Nevertheless she did, she found, after talking to him over a dinner table this evening. Like it or not, some of the impersonal quality of their relationship had gone, replaced by something rather more disturbing. Theo climbed into bed, fully expecting to lie awake worrying about it, but she fell asleep the moment her head touched the pillow.

When she opened her eyes it was daylight and early sunshine was filtering through the filmy white curtains veiling the window. Very quietly, Theo got up and put on the jade green one-piece swimsuit that had seemed such an extravagance the week before in Cheltenham, but very necessary now in Rocha do Sol, with the Villa Farol's private pool just outside the window. She tied up her hair on top of her head, snatched up a towel and went noiselessly on bare feet to open the patio doors to the morning. She threw down her towel on one of the reclining chairs by the pool and dived into the water, gasping at the coldness, then revelling in the glow that began to spread through her as she swam a few lengths of the turquoise-tiled pool before pausing for a breather. As she shook the water from her eyes in the dazzling light she realised James was watching her from the doorway, dressed in a short white towelling robe. She smiled at him cheerfully.

'Come on in,' she said breathlessly. 'It's wonderful.' A moment later she was joined by a brown, muscular body which tore through the water with an action that sent her to sit on the edge to give him room to swim. Moments later he came to her side, shaking the water from his hair and grinning at her as he heaved himself out to sit beside her, dangling his feet in the water next to hers.

'Good morning, Theodora,' he said, not even breathing hard. 'Great way to start the day.'

'Fantastic,' she agreed and jumped to her feet. 'Even better with some hot coffee to follow,' and she draped the towel over her wet swimsuit and went off to the kitchen. While the kettle was boiling Theo dressed hurriedly, and when she returned to the patio with a tray, wearing shorts and T-shirt, James was lying back in one of the chairs in his robe. He took in her fully clothed state with raised eyebrows.

'That was a very brief flash of Theodora in swimsuit! Why the urge to get dressed?'

Theo poured coffee, unruffled. 'I don't like sitting around wet.'

'Or were you afraid the sight of your half-naked body might be too much for me?'

'Of course not. I'm just more comfortable like this.' Theo untied her hair and shook it free to dry.

James sighed. 'Ah well, good thing I managed to watch you for a while before you spotted me.'

'You mean you were peeping!'

'No. Just appreciating the view. You're a pretty sight in the pool, Theodora. I'm glad I got up early.'

Theo laughed, unembarrassed by the compliment since it was delivered in such a matter-of-fact manner. They drank coffee together companionably, discussing the programme for the day, which included luncheon with José Morais and other members of the site crew, in addition to the buffet reception in the evening.

'Could we do some shopping some time?' asked Theo eagerly. 'I'd like to take back a present or two.'

He cast a lazy eye in her direction. 'For your man?'

'For my parents and aunt, actually. Presents are not possible for—for him.' Which was true enough.

James frowned. 'Can't let his wife see them, I suppose.' Distaste twisted his mouth. 'It all sounds so shabby—not good enough for you, Theodora. Can't you see that?'

Theo was growing heartily sick of her fictional lover, and changed the subject with determination.

For the rest of the day there was no time for private conversation. The morning was taken up with a detailed inspection of the site, then at a working lunch Theo recorded James's interchange with José and his staff. In the afternoon she played tennis with James, and felt half dead by the end of the second set, and only too glad of a long cold drink at the Palm Bar. Afterwards James advised a rest on her bed while he drove into Portimão with José to consult with one of the suppliers. Theo took his advice to such good effect that she woke only when James returned to shower and dress for the evening.

Theo found it decidedly strange to take a bath and wash her hair while James sang loudly in the shower of his own bathroom only a short distance away. There was an ineluctable aura of domesticity in the arrangement, she thought wryly, as his shaver buzzed in concert with her hairdryer. As she fastened her stockings and zipped up the sleek material of her new dress she could hear the clink of ice from the kitchen as James made himself a drink. The hint of intimacy made her clumsy and she took longer than usual to make up her face and brush her hair. She twisted some of the gleaming mass into a loose knot on the crown of her head and let the rest hang free, then threaded small coral-studded hoops through her earlobes, sprayed herself with perfume and gave herself a last look in the mirror. Her skin looked good against the subtle pink of the silk, even to herself, and since any doubts that a trifle too much of her skin was on display for her taste were pointless at this stage, Theo shrugged and went to join James. He was at the window in the living-room looking out to sea, a glass of whisky in his hand.

His dark, lean face took on an arrested look as he turned at the sound of her footsteps, and he continued looking at her for several moments, in a silence that made Theo uneasy.

'Will I do?' she asked at last.

'Oh yes, Theodora,' James assured her expressionlessly. 'You'll do.'

'Good.' She smiled cheerfully. 'You look rather nice yourself.'

His eyes narrowed instantly, then he grinned and gestured towards the dangling tie at the collar of his shirt. 'Are you by any chance an expert at these things? I've had to admit defeat.'

Gingerly Theo went up on tiptoe and dealt efficiently with the strip of midnight blue silk, very conscious of the warmth of his body through the thin lawn shirt he wore under his white dinner jacket. To her relief a perfect bow resulted from her first attempt, and she stood back with a triumphant smile as she viewed her handiwork.

'There. Right first time.' Her smile died as she met the intent blue eyes, and she moved back instinctively.

'Don't worry, Theodora,' James said softly. 'I won't pounce, I promise.'

'I'm glad to hear it.'

'But only because I'm aware of certain conditions.'

'My—other commitment, you mean?'

'No.' James opened the door for her. 'If I decided to

have a shot at taking you away from him a married lover would present no barrier as far as I'm concerned, I assure you. I keep my distance only because I live in mortal terror of your resignation.'

Theo nodded approvingly. 'The last bit, at least, was very sensible, Mr Hackett.'

'I thought I was James now!'

'Only while we're here. I did say *pro tem*, if you remember.'

James paused after locking the door, looking at her in reproach. 'I thought you meant until you were prepared to call me Jem.'

Theo shook her head emphatically. 'I meant until we're back in the office. Then you revert to Mr Hackett.'

'What makes you so implacable, Theodora?' he said, sighing as they walked together through the scattered white houses towards the sound of music coming from the club in the distance beyond the tree-shaded pool.

'Practical,' she corrected. 'If I were really implacable I'd have flatly refused to stay at the Villa Farol with you in the first place.'

'Why didn't you?' he asked casually.

Theo was on rather shaky ground on this point herself. 'I'm not sure,' she said with honesty, and shrugged. 'I suppose it was all the time spent as that meek mouse of a Grace, who danced to your tune without ever answering back. After the kind of treatment you dished out I suppose I find it impossible to think of you and me in an ordinary man-woman relationship.'

'While I,' said James silkily, 'am finding it easier by the minute.'

Theo glanced at him sharply, about to make a biting rejoinder, when José Morais came hurrying towards them through the groups of smartly dressed people making their way towards the clubhouse.

'Ah, James—there you are. Please hurry. Good evening, Miss Grace, how delightful you look this evening——' and at once they were swept off to join the receiving line in a flower-filled alcove just inside the restaurant, where James Hackett switched with ease to his role of man in charge, the power-house of his personality turned up full force to charm his guests, both male and female, as champagne flowed against a background of laughter and conversation and the music of a group of instrumentalists imported from Lisbon for the occasion.

Theo shook hands endlessly and smiled her most winning smile as James introduced her just as Miss Grace, with no explanation for her presence, or her function in the company. It seemed generally taken for granted she was James Hackett's lady, and since there seemed no point in making an issue with contradictions she went on smiling and doing her best to charm any likely clients interested in the purchase of the few houses still unsold.

Eventually the guests were directed to buffet tables where food was set out in a manner to delight the artistic eye as well as the gourmet palate. Theo spent a pleasant hour with Teresa Morais and several other wives of men concerned with the Rocha do Sol construction, until James returned from a conversation with the local mayor, the *prefeito*, Antonio da Silva, and swept her away to talk to various groups of British holidaymakers to sound out opinions on the accommodation and facilities.

'Everyone was quite unanimous about the place,' said Theo with a yawn, as they wandered back late to the villa. 'Absolute paradise, according to the young couple from Norwich. I think they're on their honeymoon.'

'In which case, one would assume, practically anywhere would merit the same description!' James's voice held a chuckle in the darkness.

Theo laughed. 'I suppose you're right. But most people I spoke to wanted to come again next year, and several were interested in purchasing something permanent. So I think you can take it Rocha do Sol is safely and successfully launched. Are you pleased?'

'Relieved, rather. This is my first venture outside the UK, and I've been a bit tense, I'll admit. But looking round the place now it's almost complete I'm pleased all right.'

'It has everything one could want for a holiday,' said Theo. 'Lovely climate, a spectacular beach near at hand, luxurious accommodation, swimming pools, night life at the club, tennis, a golf course ten minutes away——'

'Do you play golf?' James asked.

'No, but——'

'*He* does, I suppose!'

'Please don't start all that again—James.' His name slipped out a lot more cajolingly than Theo intended and James moved close and took her hand in his.

'Anything you say, Theodora.' To her surprise he dropped the subject at once, and discussed the evening's entertainment instead, surprising her with his capacity for detail as he commented on the food and the décor, even on some of the dresses worn by the very elegant women present.

'No one looked better than you, I might add,' he told her as they reached the villa.

Theo smiled at him warmly. 'I'm glad. Bought specially for the occasion, and it cost an arm and a leg.' She could have bitten her tongue out as she saw the look James gave her as he turned on the lights.

'In which case perhaps you'll allow me to reimburse

you for the cost,' he said suavely.

Theo turned away. 'No, thanks,' she said tightly, all her pleasure in the evening spoiled suddenly. 'I buy my own clothes.'

'Theodora, I apologise, humbly.' James caught her by the arms and turned her towards him, looking down at her with uncharacteristic contrition. 'Some of the ladies I—know,' he said slowly, 'look on the gift of a dress, or jewellery, as fairly routine. I was a fool not to realise you'd feel differently. Am I forgiven?'

Theo freed herself gently and nodded. 'Yes, of course.'

'Are you hungry?' he asked, surprising her.

She laughed, and at once the tension between them melted. 'I am a bit, now you come to mention it. I never seemed to get much opportunity for filling my plate, and, to be honest, I was afraid of getting caught with my mouth full at the wrong moment.'

'That's the problem, exactly, at these affairs, but I had the forethought to get round it very neatly.' His handsome face wore a ridiculously smug smile as he led her through the arch to the dining area. 'Dinner is served, madam,' he announced with pomp.

The table was laid out with a selection of the delicacies on display at the reception, and Theo smiled in delight. 'James—how clever! How did you arrange all this?'

'Gave one of the waiters the key and a large tip, and asked him to nip down here with a few bits and pieces before everyone devoured the lot. What do you fancy?'

'Everything!'

They filled their plates and took them into the other room to eat at leisure on one of the sofas, with a table drawn up nearby for the chilled wine James added to their haul. Theo kicked off her satin sandals and James removed his jacket and tie with a sigh of relief.

'Thank God that's over,' he said, and grinned at the sight of Theo with her feet tucked beneath her, demolishing smoked salmon canapés and turkey vol-au-vents with undisguised enthusiasm.

She smiled back, unabashed. 'Fun, isn't it? Rather like midnight feasts in the dorm at school, and all that.'

The grin James gave her was rather twisted. 'Went to a comprehensive day school myself, Miss Grace. No first-hand experience of such things, I'm afraid.'

'Neither have I. But I used to read books about boarding school. You know the sort of thing. *The Upper Fifth at St Agatha's* and so on. The girls in them never seemed to do any lessons, they were so busy rescuing each other from fires and making apple-pie beds, or scoring the winning goal at hockey for the honour of the school.'

James threw back his head and laughed. 'Not my type of literature, I'm afraid. At the same age I was probably into horror comics, or motorcycle magazines.'

'Did you ever own a motorcycle?' asked Theo with interest.

'No. It was all I could think about at one time, but I never got as far as owning one. By the time I could afford it the urge to possess one had gone.'

'Sad!'

James leaned to pour her some wine. 'What did *you* want that you've never managed to possess, Theodora?'

'A dog.'

'You mean a dog is the sum total of your ambitions?' He shook his head in disbelief. 'I can't believe that.'

'I assumed you meant something I'd longed for as a child. There are one or two things I yearn for currently, it's true,' she admitted.

The blue eyes met hers. 'Such as?'

'More food, for one,' Theo said blithely, and jumped

to her feet to restock her plate.

'You're cheating,' James complained as he followed her. 'Seriously, what else do you want that you don't actually have at the moment?'

'Independence.'

His brows came together. 'In what way?'

'I want enough money to be able to do my own thing,' she said, her eyes absent. 'To be self-sufficient, not dependent on a nine-to-five job for my bread and butter.'

James leaned against the wall, studying her. 'And how do you propose to achieve this independence of yours? Win the pools? Hope your Premium Bonds come up with the big prize?'

'Something like that. Want some of this chicken?'

He held out his plate, an odd little smile at the corners of his mouth.

'What's so funny?' she asked suspiciously.

'You and me. Playing house.'

'It *is* rather odd, I suppose,' Theo admitted when they were in the living-room again. 'I felt it earlier on when we were getting ready for the party. I felt I should have made more of a fuss about sharing with you.'

'But surely you knew you were safe with me,' he protested blandly.

'Yes, oddly enough, I did. But everyone at the party probably thought I was some sort of playmate you'd brought along for the ride!'

'Do you mind?'

'A bit.'

'I could say we're just good friends, if you like.'

Theo looked at him thoughtfully. 'But that's not altogether true either, is it? I'm just your employee, if we're being accurate.'

James stared at her broodingly. 'That doesn't preclude friendship between us, surely?'

'When you throw one of your tantrums friendship is pretty far from my feelings towards you,' she said with candour, then bit her lip. 'Too much wine—I'm sorry.'

'Don't apologise,' he said instantly. 'A case of *in vino veritas* by the sound of it.' He made a face. 'I'm not keen on the word tantrum though. Am I such a swine to work for?'

Theo was torn between a placebo and the unpalatable truth, and the latter won. 'Put it this way,' she said. 'When I went on holiday last year one of the girls from the typing pool filled in for me, right?'

'I remember,' he said bitterly. 'Utter chaos the entire time. The creature was useless. How did she get chosen to take your place, for God's sake?'

'All the girls in the typing pool drew lots. She lost.'

James stared at her aghast. 'Am I *that* bad?'

'Yes,' said Theo simply.

'So how do you cope with durance vile, then?'

'When things are bad I keep my mind firmly on my monthly pay cheque. It usually does the trick.'

'So money is your main interest.'

'No. My interest lies in what the money represents.' Theo gave a sudden involuntary yawn, and apologised. 'Sorry. Hectic day.'

James got up and collected her glass. 'You've done very well, as usual, except for the tennis, and your feeble backhand. No, seriously,' as her honey-coloured eyes flashed fire, 'my grateful thanks, Theodora.'

'All in a day's work.' Theo jumped up and stumbled awkwardly as the foot she'd been sitting on refused to support her. James fielded her neatly and held her upright, an arm round her waist.

'The wine can't be that potent!' he commented.

'My foot's gone to sleep.' Theo wiggled her numb toes, turning her face up to smile at James. Alarm bells rang in her head instantly as she saw the unfamiliar expression in the blue eyes close to hers. Theo had never seen that particular look in them before, but she knew only too well what it meant as the arm about her waist tightened and drew her close against him. She swallowed, her heart beginning to hammer.

'Please, James,' she said with difficulty. 'Please don't——'

'Don't what?' he asked, in a tone new to her, and which frightened her silly, despite its softness.

'I don't know,' she said unevenly. 'But you're making me nervous. And—and you promised you wouldn't pounce.'

'I don't think I can keep it,' he said, his voice thickening, and moved so that he held her up on her toes, just off-balance. Theo struggled to break free, but he held her easily.

James Hackett was a powerful man, with a reputation for keeping fit. Theo felt a shaming sense of helplessness in his arms, mortified that her fear of him was so obvious.

'All right,' she said suddenly in desperation. 'Do whatever it is you have to do. For heaven's sake, get it over with and let me get to bed.'

James released her with an abruptness that almost made her fall. He flung away, disgust in every line of his tall, muscular body. Theo collected her sandals, bent on escape, when he said, in a muffled voice, 'I apologise. I never intended to do that, believe me. But I touched you when you tripped, and my baser instincts suddenly took over.'

Theo stared suspiciously at his broad back. 'Forget it,' she said flatly. 'Goodnight.'

James turned sharply, his face grim. 'I'd like you to believe that I'm not usually the sort of prat who forces himself on a woman.'

'I do believe it,' she assured him drily. 'In your case I'm sure the occasion never arises.'

The tension eased in his face, and he smiled faintly. 'Not often. And the pity of it is that I was enjoying the evening very much until the "me Tarzan, you Jane" spasm overtook me.'

'So was I.'

His lips tightened. 'Sorry I blew it, Theodora.'

'As I said—forget it.' She shrugged. 'After all, we go back tomorrow. Situation normal again.'

'Ah, but will I get your resignation on my desk on Monday morning?' he asked swiftly.

'Is that all you care about?' she asked, exasperated. 'Even if I should resign, there must be dozens of women ready and able to fill my shoes any day.'

He shook his head. 'No. You're one of a kind. Who else would put up with me like you do?'

'And stay immune to those mythical charms of yours at the same time, you mean?' Theo smiled impudently. 'Personally, I just can't see what it is that bowls 'em over, you know.'

'That's what *makes* you one of a kind!' he said promptly.

'What an ego!' Theo laughed and touched his hand; James caught his hand in hers and then suddenly she was in his arms and his mouth was on hers before she could bat an eyelid. She opened her mouth to protest, but he merely held her more closely, his tongue taking advantage of her tactical error.

Utterly taken by surprise, Theo made the discovery that a kind of possession was possible by the sole medium of a kiss. His lips took and held hers with experience and a kind of leisured enjoyment that held nothing of force, only a subtle persuasion that was perilously enticing, inducing a dangerous languor in her limbs as he held her against him. A tangible driving force seemed to pass from his body to hers as his mouth evoked responses deep inside her that surprised her even more. Then, just as her mental processes belatedly gave her a sharp prod, telling her to put up some resistance, James released her and stood back, and resistance was unnecessary.

Theo looked at James dumbly, completely at a loss, conscious that some kind of protest was called for, yet only too aware that he knew perfectly well she'd enjoyed the whole thing. He put a hand to his chin, his brows drawn together in question.

'Well? Do you want me to say I'm sorry? If I did I'd be lying.'

Theo slid her feet into her shoes. 'I'm puzzled,' she said, after an interval.

'Puzzled?'

'Yes. The first time you really scared me, you know. There was such an impersonal, unreasoning look about you.'

He bit his lip. 'It's called lust, Theodora. A noncerebral type of sin to which common man is addicted.'

'Really.' Her eyes considered him gravely. 'So why wasn't I frightened the second time?'

James lifted an eloquent shoulder. 'Possibly because in some way you realised that a kiss was all I intended. And even that wouldn't have occurred if you hadn't touched me.'

'No, I know.' She flushed slightly. 'I realise it was my fault.'

'*Your* fault!' He laughed a little. 'Let's say it was no one's *fault*. Just the perfect way—or almost perfect—to round off a very enjoyable evening.'

Theo nodded matter-of-factly. 'Exactly.'

James moved towards her and she backed away

involuntarily, halting as he held up a hand, his face very
serious. 'And I give you my word you don't need to lock
your door.'

'Thank you. I'll say goodnight, then.'

'Goodnight, Theodora. Pleasant dreams.'

CHAPTER FIVE

THEO'S dreams, if any, had to have been pleasant, because she slept instantly and well. Next day, she and James swam together before breakfast; then José Morais drove them on a brief trip to Portimão before leaving. The shops of the busy port were very tempting, and Theo had no difficulty in finding gifts for her family, and was only sorry she had no more time to spend there before the return to Faro Airport and the flight home.

She and James talked desultorily but comfortably enough on the plane, with no constraint at all and Theo, faintly surprised, was relieved. The kissing had made no difference after all. In theory she would have supposed a change in their relationship inevitable, but James seemed bent on stressing that all was as before. James was no longer the indifferent autocrat of Theo's Miss Grace period, admittedly, but the more humanised version of himself she had worked with since, and she put the thought of those few bemused moments in his arms firmly from her mind.

In her efforts to reassure him that she had no intention of trading on the enforced intimacy of their stay in Portugal, Theo was more impersonal and businesslike than usual when she returned to her office the following Monday. James, after a searching look at her composed face, scowled and threw himself into routine with an irritable intensity.

Monday seemed even worse than usual, but Theo parried everything thrown at her with a serenity reinforced by thoughts of her coming interview with Diadem. Teased by Carol and the other girls on the benefits of a trip to the sun, she laughed with them, but kept the true reason for her composure firmly hidden. All week she worked furiously hard, aware that James's mood grew blacker by the day. On the Thursday she pushed herself to the limit to clear up everything possible before her day off. As she accepted the batch of mail James signed last thing Theo said goodnight, and, as an afterthought, jogged his memory about her time off the following day.

His head flew up, his brows drawn together over hard, unsmiling eyes. 'What day off?' he demanded.

Theo breathed deeply. 'The one you refused to give me *last* Friday,' she reminded him evenly.

'How about tomorrow's post?' he rapped.

'One of the girls from the pool can cope with anything urgent,' she said patiently. 'Otherwise I'll deal with it myself on Monday.'

'Friday's a hell of a day to go swanning off, Grace!'

'I didn't choose it myself. It's a business appointment.'

'In future,' he said callously, 'kindly keep your private concerns to your own time.'

Their eyes met and locked, then Theo bade him goodnight very quietly and went from the room, resisting the urge to tell her employer in great detail exactly what he could do with his rotten job. Seconds later she heard the outer door of James Hackett's office slam behind him with a crash that reverberated through the building.

Theo was nervous when she arrived at the Diadem reception desk next day. Edwardian and solid from the outside, inside the building was an ultra-modern rabbit warren of offices housed on several floors, the décor leaning to functional comfort with a good deal of potted greenery to soften the effect. She was taken up in a lift to the fourth floor and shown into an office bearing the name of Miles Hay, Editorial Director, on the door.

Miles Hay was younger than Theo had expected. He looked to be in his thirties or early forties, she thought, and was slim, with rather sleepy-looking hazel eyes and fair curly hair. He rose from behind a desk littered with manuscripts and moved round it to welcome Theo. His grasp was hard and dry, and his smile put her at her ease at once as he thanked her for coming and invited her to sit down. The telephone on his desk rang almost at once and Theo was grateful for a moment or two to get her bearings and look round the small office and at the contents of the crowded bookshelves. When Miles Hay finished his conversation he turned back to her with a friendly smile, waving a hand towards her manuscript, which lay in front of him.

'We like *The Fettered Heart*, Miss Grace,' he said without preamble. 'With a few alterations here and there I think it will do very well.'

Theo smiled at him in rapture. 'You mean it? You really *are* going to publish it?' Then she blushed, appalled at her own naïveté.

He laughed, his eyes twinkling. 'I take it this is your first literary effort, then?'

She nodded ruefully. 'It would have been my last, too, if you'd rejected it.'

'Surely you'd have kept on trying!'

'No. I would have assumed I couldn't write and given up the idea entirely. Now I can get on with the next one with more confidence.'

At once Miles Hay began questioning her on the subject matter of her next novel, then interrupted himself to suggest lunch at a restaurant within walking distance of the publishing house. The day was fine and sunny, and the short walk was pleasant. When they arrived at the restaurant they were led to a reserved table with some ceremony. Miles Hay was obviously well known to the proprietor, and waiters hovered attentively as he offered Theo a drink, which she refused.

'I'm already high from natural causes,' she said blissfully, but accepted a glass of 'designer water', as he called it, to drink with the crisp *crudités* and duck in green pepper sauce that he recommended. Excellent though it was, the food was wasted on Theo who was too excited to eat very much, as Miles Hay drew her out skilfully on her background and job, also the inspiration for her launch into the written word. She explained her addiction to reading, and her decision one day to try her hand at a novel herself, and they sat for a long time over endless cups of coffee. Eventually Miles Hay supplied her with information about royalties, publication dates and advances. Theo liked him. He had charm and a sympathetic approach towards the problems of writing, but in one way he was quite a surprise, and she told him so frankly.

'I thought you'd be a woman, Mr Hay, since you're dealing with romantic fiction.'

He laughed. 'It's more customary, I know. But in spite of my handicap of being a mere male I'm excessively clever at talent-spotting, outstandingly good at my job—and my grandfather founded the firm!'

They laughed together, Theo aware of a definite rapport between them that surprised her. Almost without realising it she found that by the time they returned to the Diadem headquarters Miles Hay knew where she lived, worked, where she went at weekends, and had even prised out of her what she hardly admitted to herself, that the man she worked for had provided the hero for her novel.

'The worst side of him, anyway,' said Theo, smiling. 'The good points are almost entirely fictional.'

Miles Hay gave her a shrewd look. 'He comes off the page as a very strong character.'

'Then I've managed to get it right.' Theo hesitated, then decided to confide in him. 'When I first started in my present job I used to arrive home at night so choked with frustrated fury I turned to writing about the cause of it as some sort of catharsis. Pouring it out on paper at night helped to keep my temper in check during the day.'

'Must be some man you work for!'

'Prides himself on being self-made and hard as nails.'

'While your Jason Harcourt is also aristocratic, subtle and ultimately irresistible.'

'Which is why it's fiction, of course!'

Theo went straight from the Diadem offices to catch a train for Cheltenham, and from the moment she arrived home until she went to bed regaled her parents with every last detail of her visit to the publishers. She was half-way up the stairs, suddenly tired after all the excitement, when Letty Grace remembered her daughter had not said a word about the trip to the Algarve.

'Oh—very enjoyable,' said Theo, offhand. 'I'll give you the presents I brought in the morning. It was hectic, but very pleasant, really. Wonderful sunshine,' and she said goodnight without enlarging further on the trip, to her parents' surprise.

Next day, Theo was back down to earth with a bump. A restless night had posed one or two awkward questions to the embryo novelist. She brought them up over lunch with her mother, while Hugh Grace was out enjoying his Saturday round of golf.

'The thing is, Mother,' she began, 'as a writer I'm not going to earn any real money for quite a while. I get an advance on publication day—which probably won't be for several months anyway, and I don't get any royalties for quite a time after that.' She sighed gloomily. 'But I know only too well that I can't continue in my job *and* write—not if I want to stay in one piece, anyway. I've already proved that. It just isn't on. But I do so badly want to write full time.'

Letty Grace smiled calmly and patted Theo's hand. 'You won't be forced to starve in a garret, darling, even if you do resign from your job. Your father and I will help willingly.'

Theo cast a doubtful look at her mother. 'But now Dad's retired surely that's not possible? Don't imagine I'll allow both of you to scrimp and save just so I can give up work!'

'Unnecessary. Your father's endowment policy is about to pay up. Quite a sizeable sum actually. More than enough to feed you *and* go on a cruise if we want.' Letty Grace looked smugly pleased with herself.

Theo's eyes filled with tears as she hugged her mother, then swabbed at her cheeks with kitchen paper. 'That's wonderful of you both, but the the problem is that I wouldn't be able to write *here*, Mother. Please don't be hurt, but it's not a very big house, and I'd never be able to concentrate with all the comings and goings with your friends. I've become rather used to my solitary attic.'

It was a problem, Mrs Grace agreed—far too sensible a lady to be hurt—but not, she assured her daugher, an insuperable one. Together they totted up Theo's assets. Her salary for the past eighteen months had been high. Her only outlay during that time had been the rent on her unshared attic studio, the prim, expensive suits bought for her role as 'Miss Grace', her food and the inevitable books. Her typewriter had been a present years ago from her father, and the paper she wrote and typed on the cheapest and flimsiest available. Every penny she could save Theo had saved.

'So you've had this in mind all along!' said her mother with a smile.

'I never even admitted to myself what I was saving

for.' Theo shook her head. 'I can't believe it even now. I keep on pinching myself to make sure it's really true.'

Letty Grace wasn't listening. She snapped her fingers suddenly. 'Of course, that's it! Edwina's cottage.'

Theo looked doubtful. 'Edwina won't want me cluttering up her dream cottage, surely?'

Her mother disagreed. Edwina had been grumbling to her sister about the high rates for the cottage and the expense of keeping it heated during cold weather, and had even talked of letting it now and then to pay for its keep.

'As a paying guest you'd be ideal. If Edwina wants the place to herself any time you can just come home,' said Mrs Grace practically. 'Your father and I will pay the rates, you can pay her some rent and possibly do a bit of gardening now and then when the muse deserts you.'

Edwina Myers was eventually tracked down next day and professed herself delighted with the proposed arrangement, and full of praise for her clever niece when she learned about the book.

'You'll miss London,' her crisp, clear voice warned.

'I'll have Ranulph for company,' said Theo jubilantly.

'I charge double for lovers!'

'Ranulph FitzRoy is the hero of my next novel, Auntie darling—Crusaders and Saracens and all that.'

'Oh well, in that case——' Edwina paused, then said slyly, 'and how about Ivan the Terrible, your belligerent boss?'

'How about him?' countered Theo airily. 'He'll just have to get someone else to slave for him.'

Despite her brave words, Theo quailed at the thought of breaking the glad news to James Hackett just the same. She spent the journey back to Chiswick trying to frame her resignation in a way that he would find acceptable, and failed dismally. Deep down she knew very well that

James would be angry, not that she harboured any illusions as to the real reason. It would not be Theodora he would miss, but 'Grace', the hard-working and efficient secretary who never complained. Girls with nice faces and hair and the required shape were easy to replace, but when those same assets were reinforced by tact, calm, excellent office skills and the ability to write and spell good English, Theo felt justified in considering herself a hard act to follow.

In the event her resignation was made unavoidable. Monday dawned bright and sunny and Theo got ready for work in a mood to match. Nothing was going to dim her glory, she decided, as she swung along through Monday morning Chiswick with a spring in her step. Having a novel accepted had wrought some alchemy in her appearance, giving an added lustre to hair and eyes, and her skin glowed, lit from within by the new confidence that added an extra dimension to her looks. And from the moment he laid eyes on her she knew James was aware of it.

His eyes narrowed and his wide, mobile mouth tightened as he watched her approach his desk. She was early, but he was earlier, and gave a significant glance at his watch as if to emphasise it. Without a pretence of greeting he plunged straight into the day's work, and Theo said nothing even though she was bitterly aware that everything from the previous Friday had been saved to add to Monday's load. For what seemed like hours she sat, pencil flying, as James rattled on at a speed meant to test her to the limit. Then, when she felt the workload was enough for any self-respecting camel's back he produced the final straw.

With a smile that was a mere show of strong white teeth he opened one of his desk drawers and produced the small machine he used for dictating at home. 'There's a report on that I roughed out yesterday,' he said casually. 'I'd like a draft of it before the end of the day—and most of the other stuff's pretty urgent. Not in a hurry to get home tonight, I trust?'

Theo stood up with her armful of papers and held out her hand for the tape recorder. 'No, Mr Hackett,' she said without emotion. 'I'll do my best to get it all finished. As usual.'

She turned on her heel and went through the communicating door without hurry, closing it behind her with extra care. Then she sat down at her electronic typewriter, fed paper into it and typed her resignation, her fingers rapping out the stark words with relish. Her earlier euphoria restored somewhat, she then began on the mammoth task James Hackett had taken such obvious pleasure in giving her. If she hadn't known better, Theo could have sworn that he was jealous of the man he believed had been the reason for her day off and her present glow. He was a dog-in-the-manger, she decided, just plain bloody-minded with pique because she was not starry-eyed over him like all the other poor creatures who came his way. Their interlude in Portugal had no doubt left him with a mistaken impression about their relationship. With determination she dismissed him from her mind and concentrated all her energies on reducing the stack of work on her desk.

James Hackett was conspicuous by his absence the entire day, to her relief, and returned to the office only when everyone in the building had gone except Theo. He went straight into his office from the corridor avoiding hers. She waited in anticipation for his reaction to her resignation, which occupied pride of place in the first compartment of the big loose-leaf file she used for letters awaiting signature. Her wait was brief. The door between their offices crashed open and James strode towards her desk, his face like thunder as he brandished her letter.

'What the hell is this?' he barked.

'My notice, Mr Hackett,' Theo replied with composure.

'The pace too much for you, I suppose,' he said cuttingly. 'Afraid of a bit of hard work!'

Her composure wavered dangerously, then stood firm enough for Theo to answer calmly, 'Not at all. If that were my reason I'd have resigned long ago.' She watched, fascinated, while James fought the rage consuming him.

'Then *why*?' he bit out at last. 'Do you want more money—I seem to recall that money's your main interest.'

'No, Mr Hackett.'

'Is it because of me—and all this?' The words seemed dragged out of him as he waved a hand at the work still remaining on Theo's desk. She went on looking at him steadily. By this time of day he always needed a second shave, and his jaw showed dark above the open collar of his white shirt. His tie dangled from the pocket of his light tweed jacket, and his hair looked as though he'd been thrusting his fingers through it all day. He returned her look, hard and penetrating, as though trying to read her mind.

Theo shook her head gravely. 'No, I'm leaving for personal reasons.'

'You're not pregnant?' he shot at her.

'Certainly not.' There was violent distaste on Theo's face as she turned pointedly to the report she was working on. 'I'm moving to the country, to be precise.'

'To live with this married lover of yours, I suppose!'

A sudden mischievous impulse seized Theo. 'No,' she said casually. 'Actually I'm involved with a different man now.'

Outrage replaced shock on James's face in a deeply satisfying manner. He flung away in disgust to his own office, slamming the door behind him, and Theo went back to her typing, a small, smug smile tugging at the corners of her mouth. James was back a few minutes later with the signed mail. He slapped it down beside her.

'Just pack this lot up and get off,' he said shortly. There was an oddly bleak look on his face as he watched her, Theo saw uneasily as she folded letters and sealed envelopes with speed. When she was finished, and her desk tidied, he was still watching her broodingly.

'I'll say goodnight then,' said Theo quietly, but he barred her way to the door, seizing her by the elbows with fingers that bruised.

'Theodora, listen to me—if you had to get involved with another man why the hell couldn't it have been me?'

Theo stared into the blue eyes, utterly astounded by their expression. Unbelievably, the man was hurt! 'You?' she repeated blankly. 'I'd never thought of you in that way, Mr Hackett.'

'For God's sake, stop calling me that!' He shook her slightly. 'You managed "James" well enough in Portugal.'

'That was purely temporary,' she said flatly, then winced as his grip tightened.

'So we're to forget everything about the trip to Rocha do Sol, are we?' he said between his teeth. 'But wouldn't this new lover of yours object a little if he knew you and I had played house for a while? Could you convince him we didn't share a bed? Will you tell him I made love to you——'

Theo wrenched herself free and stood rubbing her arms as she glared up at him. 'Since you have no idea who he is the questions don't arise. I won't talk about you. You can be sure of that. As far as I'm concerned you're not all that interesting a topic of conversation!'

'In that case,' he snarled, 'perhaps I should *make*

myself more interesting!' And without warning he threw her over his shoulder, knocking the breath out of her. Theo kicked and screamed and pummelled him frantically, but James marched through the door to the big leather chesterfield against one wall of his office and tossed her down on it, then dived on top of her, his mouth stifling her furious protests as he kept her still with one hand and wound his other tightly into her hair while he kissed her until lights danced behind her eyelids and suffocation seemed imminent. Just as Theo's lungs were at bursting point James raised his head, breathing heavily as she gasped for air.

'Let me up!' she panted malevolently, but he shook his head.

'Not until you tear up your resignation.'

'Then we'll be here indefinitely.'

'I'm not complaining.'

'James——'

'That's better!'

'Let me up—*please*!' Theo's face was pale as she pleaded, pale enough to move her captor sufficiently to sit up and let her do the same. He stared at her, his eyes grim, then jumped to his feet abruptly, raking a hand through his hair.

'I'm sorry,' he said jerkily. 'I must have been mad.'

Wearily Theo got up, smoothing down her skirt and tucking her shirt into the waistband. Her mouth felt bruised and sore, and when she touched an experimental finger to her lip it came away with blood on it. All at once she felt tired enough for tears, and had to exert iron control to keep them back.

'Why aren't you running away?' asked James.

'Because I'm almost too tired to walk,' she retorted bitterly.

Swiftly he moved towards her and put a hand beneath her chin, wincing as he saw the trickle of blood from her lip. 'Not much of a hand at gentle persuasion, am I, Theodora? What *is* it with you? First, you're all but invisible, a perfect, uncomplaining shadow of a secretary. Now you're all I can think about! Why the hell do you think I'm such a swine to work for these days?'

'You've always *been* a swine to work for.' With her resignation in his possession Theo saw no need to pull her punches any more.

'I mean, since we got back from the Algarve,' he said shortly. 'After our brief stay under the same roof I just can't seem to adjust to an impersonal relationship. I thought we'd become friends over there, dammit—and *more* than friends, if I'm honest. Then the Monday we got back Theodora had vanished and Grace was back. Minus the glasses, but Grace just the same, with her "Yes, Mr Hackett" and "No, Mr Hackett", which meant "As you were, holiday over".'

Theo shrugged. 'I thought you'd prefer it that way. Surely you didn't want me referring to you as James and making coy little references to our trip in front of your staff?'

'True. But I didn't expect a return to hostilities, either. I was under the impression we'd established some kind of peace between us.'

'Peace! I'm afraid I associate war with you more readily!'

'I'd rather make love than war, Theodora.' The blue eyes darkened as he moved closer, and Theo retreated hurriedly.

'The sole reason for your sudden interest in me is my lack of it in *you*,' she said flatly. 'To you I'm a challenge. Not Theo Grace, an ordinary girl who happens to work for you, but the one who got away.'

James shook his head emphatically. 'Not true. Listen to me. Please, Theodora.'

Unwillingly Theo nodded. 'Very well, but could you

make it brief, please. It's late.'

'This man you're moving in with,' he began. 'Have you known him long?'

'No.'

'What kind of place is he providing for you?'

Theo looked away guiltily. 'It's a cottage in the Cotswolds,' she muttered.

'Whereas I could offer you a luxury apartment not far from here, with a view of the river, full hotel services, done out throughout by an interior designer——'

'You mean *share* it with you?' she interrupted, aghast.

'Naturally.' James's face set in tense lines.

'There's nothing natural about it,' she said scornfully. 'You mean I work myself into the ground here by day and then trot off to your cosy little den in the evenings to cook your dinner and entertain you in bed afterwards as the *pièce de résistance*? You've got to be joking!'

'I'm not, you know. I'd accept your resignation gladly if you'd fulfil the last part of the programme only. I'll find another secretary somewhere, and meals can be sent in.' James moved closer. 'Is it so impossible to contemplate, Theodora?'

'Being your mistress?'

'No. I meant living together.'

Theo's eyes flashed fire. 'No you don't. You mean sleeping together. What would I do every day until bedtime? Study the necessary textbooks to become more proficient at the art of pleasing you?' Her scorn brought dark, angry colour to James's lean face.

'You're twisting my words——'

'Not really. The message seems fairly plain to me.' She shook her head. 'I'm afraid your offer doesn't tempt me in the slightest, James Hackett.'

In silence he stared for long moments into her hostile face, then with a smothered curse he reached for her and kissed her hard, jerking her against him as though the end of his tether had been reached and passed. Too weary to resist by now Theo let him do as he wanted, depending on her sheer passivity to deter the frustrated emotion he was expending on trying to win some response from her. But after a time his determination proved too much for her resistance. To her shame she felt a flicker of response come to life somewhere deep inside her and her lips softened involuntarily. Instantly she could feel the triumph ignite in the hard body pressed against hers. Through their clothes she could feel the coiled tension of his desire, and some primitive response to it woke within her. Instantly there was fire that licked at her and made her gasp and twist beneath caressing, expert fingers that sought and found the vulnerability of the body that curved into his instead of staying rigid in opposition.

Then, unbelievably, she was returning his kisses, her breathing now as ragged as his, and James was saying her name brokenly, over and over again, a fevered litany of persuasion against her lips as he drew her down with him to the sofa once more, this time with cajoling hands and lips and body as, gently, he smoothed open the fastenings of her shirt so his lips could learn the generous contours of her breasts, which lifted, their nipples hardening under the enticement of his mouth.

'Is that you, Mr Hackett?' said a voice outside the door, then it opened and the security officer stood there appalled for an instant before he disappeared in a hurry at James's snarled curse. Theo leapt to her feet in an agony of shamed embarrassment, running for the connecting door and scooping up her handbag from the floor where she had dropped it during James's caveman tactics. Sobbing with disgust she flew to the washroom, spashing her face with cold water. She rebuttoned her shirt with fingers that shook and combed her hair into some kind of order, feeling physically sick. When she finally emerged James was waiting for her, his face set in grim lines that made him look years older.

'I leave on Friday,' said Theo bluntly. 'I would leave now, but I have enough principle to feel I can't leave you without trying to find you a replacement. '

'Don't do me any favours,' he said grimly. 'You can leave right now, as far as I'm concerned. After all, I've proved my point.' He jerked his head towards his office door. 'Back there I established one thing beyond all question. You're no more immune to me than anyone else, Theodora.'

She fairly shook with rage. 'So now you've conducted your shabby little experiment to your own satisfaction——'

'Not quite that, unfortunately.' His chuckle set her teeth on edge. 'Miller interrupted us before I got to that point.'

Theo brushed past him and went into her office. Quickly and methodically she emptied the desk of her private belongings, tipping everything into a polythene carrier bag. James watched her from the doorway in silence, but she carried on as if he wasn't there, until the desk was pin-neat and she was ready to leave.

'Where shall I send the money owing to you?' he asked as he moved aside for her to pass. Theo would have given much to refuse his money, but common sense told her she would need it in the near future and she was forced to pocket her pride.

'Have it sent to my present address,' she said coldly. 'Charlie Cowper will forward it to me.'

'Ah, the passionate landlord. Of course.' His irony was blistering, but by this stage Theo was immune.

'Goodbye,' she said numbly, and walked past him towards the lift. James reached it before her and followed her in to go down to the foyer. As the lift gave a lurch at the start of its descent Theo's stomach followed suit and suddenly she found it hard to breathe in the airless confines of the cubicle. Perspiration broke out on her forehead, lights danced in front of her eyes, then everything went black as she tumbled into nothingness.

When Theo came to she was lying on a sofa again. This time it was chintz-covered and vaguely familiar and she looked up from it into the three faces bending over her, Nicola and Charlie Cowper and James Hackett.

With soothing little sounds of relief and comfort Nicola propped her up while Charlie held a glass of ice-water to her lips. Theo sipped gratefully, her eyes on James's set, ashen face.

'There you are, old love,' said Charlie kindly, so kindly Theo's eyes filled with tears and Nicola held her close, mopping her up with tissues.

'What happened?' asked Theo huskily, when she had herself in hand.

'You fainted in the lift at Turnham Green, so I loaded you into my car and brought you here,' James informed her briefly. 'Cowper suggested I bring you in here when I rang the bell, rather than carry you up to your own room.'

'Goodness, yes,' said Nicola fervently. 'He might have dropped you, or anything.'

Charlie grinned. 'And since our Theo's a fine figure of a girl, darling, there's a possibility the chap might have done himself an injury by the time he got up four flights of stairs, too.'

'How do you feel?' James asked Theo quietly.

Absolutely spiffing, thought Theo, but managed some sort of smile. 'Better,' she said aloud. Which was a lie.

'Did you skip lunch or something today?' demanded Nicola accusingly.

'Yes. Didn't have time.' Theo took a detached

pleasure in watching James's lips compress. 'Busy day today.' And wasn't *that* the truth!

'Let me whip up something,' said Nicola instantly.

'No—no, really.' Theo got up groggily, wavering slightly and James put out an instinctive hand to steady her. She looked pointedly at the strong fingers on her arm until they were removed, then smiled brightly at the Cowpers. 'I'll open a tin or whatever, then fall into bed.'

'It's only nine o'clock, love,' protested Charlie.

'Is that all?' said Theo in surprise. 'It feels like midnight.'

'I'll see you up the stairs,' said James, something in his face deterring Charlie from any argument. Theo, too feeble to voice further protest, thanked the Cowpers and let herself be shepherded firmly from the flat.

It was a trying ascent to the attic floor. For one thing Theo felt quite terrible, and for another she was burningly conscious of the inexorable hand under her elbow as James helped her up the stairs in oppressive silence. By the time they had reached the second floor landing James had had enough.

'Despite your landlord's doubts about my capabilities,' he said with irony, 'I think you need a lift.' And he swung Theo up in his arms and carried her slowly and carefully up the remaining stairs. 'You never mentioned that there was a Mrs Cowper, by the way,' he remarked as he set her on her feet at her door.

'Should I have done?' It didn't seem in the least important to Theo. Nothing did except the urge to get to bed. She fumbled with her key, and James took it from her and unlocked the door.

'May I come in?' he asked.

Theo stared at him blankly. 'No,' she said, and tried to shut the door in his face. James stuck out a handsome brown leather shoe and prevented her.

'I'm deeply sorry, Theodora.' His face was devoid of

any expression so it was difficult to know what he was sorry for.

'Are you?' she said, without much interest.

'I didn't mean what I said.'

'You said a lot of things.'

'I meant that I very much want you to live with me and share my life. The bit about your being like all the rest was just——'

'One of your tantrums.'

'If you must put it like that, yes.'

Theo regarded him with detachment, thinking how imposing a figure he made on the narrow landing, dark and formidable in the late evening light.

'James,' she said tiredly. 'I've mapped out my life very tidily for the time being. There's no place in it for you. I know that tonight you proved I'm as vulnerable to your form of sexual persuasion as the next woman. In fact, another few minutes and the scene Miller would have interrupted would have been a great deal more embarrassing all round. *In flagrante delicto* is the term, I believe. Part of your anger afterwards was due to frustration, I suppose. Just as my ultimate cave-in was the result of shocked self-revelation on top of a twelve-hour working day with no break for lunch.'

James breathed in sharply. 'Twisting the knife, Theodora!'

'Not at all. What I'm trying to say is that whatever you want of me I can't give it. I have other things to do with my life.'

'And other men to do them with,' he added harshly.

'Yes.' Theo felt no compunction at her half-truth. Jason Harcourt, Ranulph FitzRoy, even Miles Hay; they were all men she was involved with to some extent.

'Then this is it, Theodora,' said James heavily.

'Yes, James. Goodbye. Thank you for bringing me home.'

'Since I was directly responsible for your collapse it seemed the least I could do.'

His bleak blue eyes held hers in a silence that stretched Theo's nerves to breaking point, then, at last, James gave her an oddly formal bow and turned to make the long descent to the ground floor. Theo remained where she was, spent and motionless, listening to his footsteps until the outer door of Willow Lodge closed far below with a finality that left her with a chill, unexpected feeling of regret.

CHAPTER SIX

EDWINA MYERS had spent a lot of money on Honeysuckle Cottage, which was one of a row of four once
owned by the nearby manor house in Bedington, a few
miles from Chipping Campden. Now the big house was
a private hotel and the labourers' cottages occupied only
at weekends or holidays by people whose lives, like
Edwina's, were spent in the city.

Theo loved the small house on sight. It was the end
cottage, more or less like the others, with the steeply
pitched roof and pointed gables characteristic of the
area. In winter the stone walls could look greyish, but
one ray of sunshine was enough to gild them to the
famous honey-coloured Cotswold glow. High hedges
separated the gardens, but privacy was hardly necessary,
since for most of the time Theo was the solitary
occupant of all four cottages. They were reached by
means of an unadopted road, a loose description for
dusty ruts in summer and axle-high mud in the winter
for those with wheels. Theo's only wheels were on the
bicycle owned since she was at school, and when she
needed odds and ends she pedalled into Bedington, or
occasionally as far as Chipping Campden, but otherwise
depended on a weekly visit from her parents with the
staples they insisted on providing as their share of
patronage for the struggling young novelist.

Edwina breezed into Theo's life some weekends, full
of the hustle and bustle of her own life, and sometimes
her niece felt a decided pang of nostalgia when she
listened to Edwina's accounts of theatre trips and

concerts, but it was fleeting, and generally assuaged by the books Edwina never failed to bring with her.

Research was easy at Honeysuckle Cottage. Theo could bury herself in it, and scatter books around her in ever-increasing circles, serene in the knowledge that they could stay there in chaos until she finished with them. She worked in her small bedroom on the pine end of the cottage, near the window with the view of undulating hills and the roofs of Bedington Manor Hotel just visible above a fold of green meadow in the distance. At first the quiet had been dismayingly oppressive, but after a month or two Theo grew used to it, hugging the silence to her as a friendly aid to concentration.

The Fettered Heart had been revised, the proofs corrected, and publication was scheduled for just before Christmas, much earlier than Theo had dared to hope. Of James she thought as little as possible, which meant she thought of him far more than she would have liked. Their final, stormy encounter lingered on in Theo's mind persistently, and to exorcise the memory she used the experience, writing about it in her book with ruthless objectivity, making it into a fiery passage between her hero, Ranulph FitzRoy, and the object of his desire, the Lady Adelise. Ranulph was on Crusade against the Saracens and Theo ran up against a problem she would never have envisaged possible before starting to write. Her characters sometimes refused to do what she wanted. So much so that twelfth-century Adelise, captured by Khair-ad-din, the Saracen enemy, found his swarthy, sinuous charms preferable to the red-gold hair and blunt approach of Ranulph FitzRoy. Eventually Ranulph was forced to kill the Saracen in combat before the lady was restored to him, but even then the stubborn Adelise spurned his advances so firmly that he was obliged to pay court to her more assiduously than

Ranulph, a man of his times, felt strictly necessary, since in the eyes of their insular world she was considered second-hand goods.

Two letters came from James Hackett soon after Theo moved into Honeysuckle Cottage, both of them forwarded by Charlie Cowper. The first was a stark apology, and enclosed a very generous cheque purporting to be holiday money and various other payments due to his former secretary. Blood money, thought Theo, who wrote a terse thank-you letter and banked the cheque. The second letter had a tinge of austere appeal that touched her in some strange way. He knew his behaviour had been unforgivable, James wrote, but hoped it was not a barrier to some kind of friendship between them in the future. He would like to see her if ever she was in London, he went on, and ended by asking her to remember him if ever she was in need.

Of what? Theo wondered. Did he picture her as lonely and abandoned by her apocryphal lover? She felt she should laugh, but put the letter away unanswered for the simple reason she could think of no answer to make. Soon afterwards she forgot it in her excitement at the arrival of a parcel containing complimentary copies of her novel. Theo stared at the cover in rapture. It was on the lurid side, admittedly, with a *décolletée* lady clasped in the arms of a man on horseback at the foot of an embattled tower silhouetted against a colourful sunset, but the author was charmed. *The Fettered Heart* by Theodora Grace, was there in bold letters for all the world to see, and she danced a jig round the parlour of the cottage before rushing to the telephone to let her parents know the glad news.

Edwina was bringing a guest for the weekend, a man friend, and Theo would be *de trop*, her aunt had informed her, so Hugh Grace collected his daughter

Say  to

romance

Say yes to free gifts worth over $15.00

Say YES to a rendezvous with romance, and you'll get 4 classic love stories—FREE! And you'll get a delightful surprise—FREE! These gifts carry a total value of over $15.00—but you can have them without spending even a penny!

MONEY-SAVING HOME DELIVERY!

Say YES to Harlequin's Home Reader Service® and you'll enjoy the convenience of previewing 8 brand-new books every month, delivered right to your home before they appear in stores. Each book is yours for only $1.99—26¢ less than the retail price, and there is no extra charge for postage and handling.

SPECIAL EXTRAS—FREE!

You'll get our newsletter, *heart to heart*, packed with news of your favorite authors and upcoming books—FREE! You'll also get additional free gifts from time to time as a token of our appreciation for being a home subscriber.

Say yes to a Harlequin love affair. Complete, detach and mail your Free Offer Card today!

Get your fabulous gifts
ABSOLUTELY FREE!

Hᴀʀʟᴇǫᴜɪɴ ʜᴏᴍᴇ ʀᴇᴀᴅᴇʀ sᴇʀᴠɪᴄᴇ®

FREE OFFER CARD

4 FREE BOOKS   **FREE DELIVERY**

Place YES
sticker here

**FREE FACT-FILLED
NEWSLETTER**   **FREE SURPRISE**

Please send me 4 Harlequin Presents® novels, free,
along with my surprise gifts as explained on the
opposite page.

108 CIH CANE

Name _____
       (PLEASE PRINT)

Address _____ Apt _____

City _____

State _____ Zip _____

Offer limited to one per household and not valid for present subscribers.
Prices subject to change.   PRINTED IN U.S.A.

next day for a long weekend at home in Cheltenham, hugging her when he saw her book for himself. The rejoicing was increased ten-fold when Theo spotted her novel in the historical romance section of a large book shop during a shopping session with her mother over the weekend.

'Now I know it's real,' she breathed, staring at it in rapture.

'Very real,' hissed her mother. 'Look—that girl over there is buying a copy!'

There had been some letters waiting for Theo when she arrived home. One of them was from Charlie Cowper. James Hacket had been to Willow Lodge, demanding to know Theo's whereabouts.

'Didn't quite know what to do,' wrote Charlie, 'but Nicola felt we'd better give him your parents' address at least, so perhaps they can field any approaches from him. It just didn't seem possible to refuse the man, somehow—persistent blighter. Hope we haven't been crassly indiscreet, love.'

Theo looked up sharply at her mother. 'Has anyone contacted you trying to find out where I am?'

Letty Grace shook her head. 'Anyone in particular?'

'James Hackett.' Theo told her what Charlie had written.

'And what am I supposed to do if he does get in touch?' demanded her mother. 'I'm not awfully fond of lying.'

'I know. You're hopelessly bad at it, too.' Theo sighed, not a little ruffled at hearing about James. The very mention of his name reminded her of things she preferred to forget. 'Just tell him I insist on keeping my address secret, Mother. I've no intention of working for him again, which can be the only possible reason for his wanting to see me.'

Letty Grace looked unconvinced. Theo had given only the sketchiest account of her precipitate departure from Hackett Construction, so plainly preferring not to discuss James Hackett at all that her parents had abided by her unspoken plea for silence. Nevertheless her mother had her own private ideas on the subject.

'Perhaps he just wants to see you socially,' she said with care.

'Most unlikely.' Theo got up to make coffee and the subject was tacitly dropped.

Theo had been back at the cottage before she allowed herself to think about James. In the beginning, during her first days there, she had done her best to pretend he didn't exist, with varying success. Sometimes those last few moments in his office, coiled together in a breathless frenzy, had a way of cropping up very vividly in her mind and, to her infinite shame, in her body. She was outraged that she could have responded with such abandon to someone she wasn't sure she even liked. Not that liking was necessary for physical chemistry, Theo was well aware. And, to be honest with herself, it had been easy to see why women found James attractive. Their trip to the Algarve had made that clear enough. No one could have been better company, and except for one memorable episode he had even refrained from taking advantage of their enforced intimacy at the Villa Farol, which must have been foreign to his normal course of action with a woman.

Pity he's such a pig to work for, Theo thought regretfully. Lord knew what he'd be like to live with. All very well going to bed with an exciting lover, but the thought of waking up to James Hackett as only his secretary knew he could be, acid, ruthless and overbearing, was hardly a prospect to tempt any sensible woman. And yet, to her infinite surprise, she missed him. I'm

like Bill Sikes's dog, Theo concluded in disgust, and
thrust thoughts of James away to concentrate on
Ranulph FitzRoy instead. He, at least, was forced to
dance to her bidding—most of the time.

Christmas was rapidly drawing near, Theo realised,
when she was curled up in front of the fire, watching
snippets of forthcoming Yuletide programmes on the
television. Some shopping would be necessary very
soon, if she were to avoid a frantic last-minute scramble.
The holiday period would be spent in Cheltenham, as
usual, and promised to be quieter than normal this year,
since lucky old Edwina was off skiing with her new man.

Theo felt a pang of envy. Edwina was so sure of herself
and what she wanted from life. No marriage for Edwina
Myers. Domesticity had no place in her scheme of things
at all. Not, thought Theo with a grin, that men were
excluded from Edwina's life, by any means; quite the
reverse. The latest beau was quite something, apparently, a brilliant QC, and sexy with it, to quote Edwina.
Theo sighed, conscious that for the time being at least,
she had cut herself off from male company entirely, and
consoled herself with images of *The Fettered Heart*
snapped up by thousands of Christmas shoppers for
presents.

Next day the weather decided it was winter at last, and
spattered showers of sleet against the windows of
Honeysuckle Cottage. For weeks it had been foggy and
mild, but now the wind had a bite and the sky looked
yellow-grey with the threat of snow. Theo ignored the
elements and plunged deep into the absorbing task of
joining Ranulph in marriage to the fiery, rebellious
Adelise. Scribbling away furiously, transported back to a
world of flickering torchlight and rush-strewn stone
floors in a great hall where wine-sodden wedding guests
grew more raucous and bawdy by the minute, Theo was

recalled to the present with an effort by the sound of the telephone. She careered down the steep, narrow stairs and grabbed the receiver with a breathless 'hello'.

'I was just about to ring off,' said a pleasant, drawling voice and Theo frowned, puzzled.

'Charlie?' she said uncertainly.

An amused chuckle answered her. 'Sorry to disappoint you, Miss Grace. I'm afraid it's Miles Hay.'

'No disappointment at all, Mr Hay,' Theo assured him, delighted. 'I was knee-deep in the twelfth century. Modern miracles like the telephone take rather a time to penetrate when the flow is flowing.'

'I'm happy to hear it. I rang to ask what you thought of *The Fettered Heart* in the flesh, so to speak?'

'Fantastic! I actually saw someone buying a copy in Cheltenham.'

'I'm sure a great many other people will follow suit.' There was a pause. 'I wondered if you'd fancy sparing the time for a trip to London for a celebratory lunch?'

Would she! Theo's eyes sparkled as she told him she'd love to. 'I'll come early and get in a spot of Christmas shopping,' she added. 'Thanks very much, Mr Hay.'

'How about calling me Miles?'

'Fine. I'm Theo usually.'

'Not Theodora?'

'No!' she said vehemently. 'I mean, I prefer Theo.'

'Then Theo it shall be.'

Miles Hay named a restaurant and a time to meet him there the following day and Theo put down the receiver feeling very pleased with life. A day in London was quite a treat after her ultra-quiet life in Bedington, and she looked forward to seeing Miles again, too. It would be very pleasant to lunch with an attractive man in a smart restaurant like Le Château, a definite improvement on the usual cheese sandwich munched as she read through the morning's output.

Later that evening Theo gave Edwina a ring. 'Auntie darling, can I borrow something to wear? There's a rather yummy jacket in your wardrobe.' She went on to explain about her lunch date and Edwina, in her usual generous way, told her niece to help herself to anything she liked.

'I fancy I left a brown leather skirt there, too, Theo. I usually wear that with the paprika wool jacket, and there's a gold paisley wool shirt with an outsize bow tie that goes with it. Have a great time with your literary gent, then, and not too much tiddly with the meal.'

'You're a doll, Edwina—thanks,' said Theo fervently, and spent the rest of the evening catching up on the finer points of grooming that went by the board when her prose was coming off the pencil in full spate.

It was wonderful to be back among London crowds and traffic again Theo found, as, feeling dashing in her borrowed plumes, she revisited her old haunts in South Molton Street for a spot of window shopping and went to Fenwick's to stock up on warm, jewel-coloured socks and tights. She had found out the hard way that writing for hours on end resulted unromantically in cold feet. Theo enjoyed herself so much, just browsing through the goodies on display, that she was a little late arriving at the restaurant in Stratton Street. She was led straight to a downstairs table where Miles rose at her approach and relieved her of her parcels, his eyes frankly appreciative as they took in her glowing face and casual, elegant clothes.

'You look marvellous, Theo,' he said warmly, after the greetings were over. 'I like the outfit.'

'Borrowed from my maiden aunt,' said Theo honestly, and he laughed.

'I thought you'd been on a spree and spent your advance!'

'No fear—nothing so improvident.' Theo relaxed in her chair, enjoying the silver mug of Pimms the waiter brought her and looking about her with pleasure at the crowded room. The muted sound of sophisticated piano music came from the bar and she gave a sigh of satisfaction. 'This is *so* nice, Miles.'

'You've not been here before?' His sleepy eyes were indulgent as she shook her head.

'I've made reservations here a few times for the man I used to work for, but places like this are above a poor secretary's touch, you know.'

'May I remind you that you're a published writer now, Theo. I'm confident you'll be able to eat where you like very soon.'

Much cheered by this, Theo ordered from the menu with gusto, then looked across at her companion. Miles Hay looked very urbane and polished in a dark, beautifully cut suit, with a discreet foulard tie at the collar of his fine cambric shirt. His hands, as they toyed with his glass of Tio Pepe, were long and slim-fingered, and looked as though they'd never done anything more demanding than move a chess piece or sign a cheque. 'Did you ask me to lunch for any particular reason?' she asked.

'Why, yes. I wanted to see you again.'

'Oh. I thought maybe you wanted to discuss something with me, about the book I'm working on now, maybe.'

'That too, but I also wanted the pleasure of your company for a while.' He glanced round him and smiled warmly. 'In common with most other men in the room, at a rough guess.'

Theo felt absurdly pleased, and settled down to enjoy

herself to the full, dispensing firmly with a first course to leave room for the exquisite chocolate mousse that followed her salmon in watercress sauce. Miles was a witty, entertaining companion and very easy to talk to, Theo found, as she gave him a run-down on the progress of the new novel so far, accepted with gratitude a few helpful suggestions on the storyline and even ventured a few questions about her host in return as they lingered over coffee after the meal.

'I would have run down to Gloucestershire and chanced a welcome at your little retreat, but decided against it,' Miles informed her. 'Since I gather your whereabouts are concealed from the world at large I assumed you were wary of intruders.'

'You wouldn't be an intruder, Miles,' she assured him. 'Come any time you like. It's a bit off the beaten track, but if you care to make the journey I'd be very pleased to see you.'

'I may take you up on that,' he said absently, his eyes looking past her shoulder. 'Theo, I may be imagining it, but there's a man a few tables away whose eyes are fixed on the back of your head. You're easy to look at, I grant you, but this chap doesn't seem able to take his eyes off you.'

'Must think I'm Edwina,' said Theo, resisting the urge to turn round in her seat and investigate. 'We have the same colour hair, and these *are* her clothes.'

Miles grinned. 'Possibly. I rather fancy the lady with him is showing signs of rebellion, though—quite definitely not the type used to her escort's showing interest in other women.'

'You're making me *very* curious. I'll pop off to powder my nose so I can have a casual look on the way back to the table.'

The dining-room was divided into three by stone

arches, and as Theo, hair smoothed and face refurbished, made her way back to Miles she discovered, with shock, just who was taking such an interest in her. As she walked without hurry to her seat she had a partial view of the back of Chloë Masson's blonde head and fur-clad shoulders, and a head-on confrontation with James Hackett in the moody, magnificent flesh. Theo smiled at him coolly, answered by a feral glare that made her sit down rather abruptly in the chair Miles held out for her.

'So you know him,' stated Miles, as he sat down.

'Yes. I was his PA for eighteen months until I departed for a full-time career in writing.'

'From the look on his face would I be right in thinking you parted with him on fairly unamicable terms?'

'Yes. He wasn't exactly thrilled when I resigned.'

'Does he know the reason?'

'No, I never told anyone in the company about my writing.'

'So what does he think you're doing with yourself now?'

'I told him I was going to live in the country with a man,' said Theo, grinning.

Miles blinked. 'May I ask who?'

'Ranulph FitzRoy, of course—not that I felt it necessary to explain!'

The indolent eyes became searching. 'Then the gentleman's interest is not entirely professional, I gather?'

Theo looked down into her refilled coffee-cup. 'James is the sort of man who's used to women making fools of themselves over him. His particular brand of sledgehammer charm isn't my cup of tea, that's all.'

'Ah! I see.' Miles grinned. 'Can't say I blame him for feeling annoyed. So would I if I'd had a secretary like you. Mine is totally enamoured of her husband, ungrateful creature!'

Theo smiled abstractedly. 'Is James still there?'

'Afraid so.' Miles glanced at his watch apologetically. 'And I'm due at a meeting shortly. We'll just have to run the gauntlet, Theo. Do we sweep out regally, ignoring the chap, or have a cosy little chat en route?'

The decision was made for them, since James rose to his feet, blocking the way as they reached his table.

'Hello, Theodora,' he said coldly, and turned to Miles. 'Won't you introduce me?'

'Of course,' said Theo, resigned. 'Miles Hay, James Hackett.'

The men gave each other a brief nod of acknowledgement, then a plaintive, throaty voice said, 'What about me, darling? Don't *I* get a mention?'

James looked at the beautiful, fair face of his companion blankly, as though he'd forgotten who she was, and Miles hastily stepped into the breach, introducing himself, bending to hear what she was saying, and James drew Theo a little way apart.

'How are you?' he asked quietly.

'Very well. And you?' Theo could hardly believe this was happening. It all seemed so unreal, the chatter of diners lingering over their meals, the piano music in the background, and James's steely blue eyes locked with hers as he ignored her question.

'Cowper gave me a Cheltenham address, under duress,' he said.

'He told me. It's my parents' home.'

'Give me your own address, Theodora—*please!*'

'No, James.' Theo met his eyes levelly and his lips tightened. He glanced at Miles, who was making polite conversation with the vivacious Chloë. 'Is he——?'

'No.'

'No! How many men do you need, for God's sake!'

The words were in a bitter undertone, but Miles glanced up sharply, hearing the tone if not the words, and after a look at Theo's face came to take her arm.

'Time we were off, Theo, I think,' he said smoothly and nodded courteously to the other two. 'Nice to meet you both. Goodbye.'

James looked dangerous for a moment then stepped back, allowing them to pass.

'Goodbye.' Theo included Chloë in the stiff smile she managed as they left, but James said nothing at all, and Theo felt his eyes on her back until they were outside in the cold December afternoon.

'That was interesting,' remarked Miles. 'Are you all in one piece, Theo?'

'More or less. Sorry about all that.' Theo felt limp with reaction.

'I wouldn't like to get on the wrong side of *that* gentleman!' Miles smiled at her with sympathy.

'James is still annoyed with me, it seems,' she said lightly.

'Annoyed! My dear girl, the man was so jealous he could hardly see straight!'

Theo went scarlet and dropped one of her packages. By the time Miles restored it to her she had herself in hand again and thanked him for the lunch.

'The pleasure was mine. I rather enjoyed the cabaret, too,' he added wickedly. 'Particularly when it dawned on me I was actually meeting your Jason Harcourt in person, black hair, blue eyes, the lot.'

'It's off with the old and on with Ranulph FitzRoy now,' declared Theo and held out her hand. 'Goodbye, Miles.'

'Goodbye, Theo. I'll be in touch, and you know where I am if you run into any difficulties with the book.

Where are you bound now? There's a taxi if you want it.'

'Great! I'm for Harrods and then back to my bolthole—far more peaceful than the big city!'

Theo almost skipped her Christmas shopping, then rallied herself sharply, glad of the taxi-ride to get over the shock of seeing James again. Fate was obviously in festive mood to send her to lunch at a place James patronised, though she would hardly have expected him to waste precious time on a social lunch date midweek. Perhaps it had been some special occasion, she thought bleakly, and tipped the taxi driver far too lavishly in her abstraction when she arrived in Knightsbridge.

Much of her pleasure in her day out had evaporated, and she bought her presents quickly, not even lingering in the book department as long as usual. Yet back in the cottage the quiet seemed almost menacing when the taxi had gone and she was alone in the house. Theo hurriedly switched on lights and turned up the heating, then made herself a quick snack to eat while talking to her mother on the telephone for company, giving her a resumé of the day in London, including the encounter with James.

'That must have been rather startling, darling,' said Letty with sympathy.

Theo agreed, but quickly changed the subject to her glamorous lunch and her shopping spree. Bother James, she thought angrily later. Nothing on television interested her, she found, and for once she had difficulty in losing herself in the pages of a book. It was useless to pretend that meeting James had left her unaffected, because she knew only too well that this restless, irritable feeling stemmed from seeing him again. His face kept coming between her eyes and the printed page, looking more haggard than when she'd seen it last. James was the one with circles under his eyes now, and there were new lines at the corners to match those at his mouth, and, unbidden, a bleak feeling of anxiety prodded at her. Perhaps he was ill. In which case he would hardly have been lunching at Le Château with Chloë Masson, she reminded herself acidly, and took herself to bed.

Next day, to her relief, Theo felt less unsettled, and after a few necessary chores, spent the day on her book, with a percolator of coffee at her elbow as she worked. Some necessary revision on her research took up the entire evening afterwards, and gradually Theo managed to restore James Hackett to his normal place, firmly shut away in the back of her mind. The weekend brought Edwina in a flurry of excitement over her forthcoming skiing trip, showing off the new gear bought for it and exclaiming in delight over the elegant *après-ski* sweater Theo had bought her for Christmas.

'Darling—what you must have paid for it, you naughty thing!'

'I make it a habit to keep in with my landlords. While I was in Harrods I ordered a case of wine for the Cowpers, since they're so good at playing postmen for me.'

'Nice day in London?' Edwina was still eyeing herself happily in the mirror, holding the brilliant peacock greens and blues of the sweater against her.

'Tiring, but fun. Your outfit went down well with my editor, by the way—*and* with James Hackett, you may care to know.'

Edwina dropped the sweater in astonishment. '*Really*? Tell Auntie all about it.'

Theo grinned as 'Auntie', in a white mohair sweater and black cord jeans, sat down on the arm of the sofa, one leg swinging impatiently as she listened. Her dark eyes widened as Theo gave an account of the incident.

'Darling,' said Edwina afterwards, 'are you sure you

don't have just a tiny suspicion of a *tendre* for your terrible tyrant?'

Theo looked away. 'No.'

'I suspected as much. So why cut him out of your life altogether?'

Theo was a long time answering. 'The thing is, Edwina,' she said at last slowly. 'He's the sort of man who doesn't give one room. I mean, if I allowed him any kind of place in my life I honestly believe he'd try to taken over completely. And I want to write. I love writing, Edwina—I love losing myself in the lives of the characters I create. And now, by some miracle, I've actually been published, I want to go on, to improve, to polish and develop any talent I have.'

Edwina nodded slowly. 'I can understand that. Who better? But——' she hesitated delicately, 'I've never made any secret of the fact that although I'm not keen on sharing my life with a man, I'm not averse to a spot of social life with one. You, on the other hand, are living a vicarious sort of life through your characters. Your book was great, Theo—I loved it. I kept on thinking "My little niece has written this" all the time I was reading it, and I'm very proud of you. But you need a bit of first-hand experience now and then, you know, if only to provide research for the love scenes. Mind you, that Jason Harcourt of yours was distinctly naughty in places—unmentionable ones at that! Made me see you in a new light, I can tell you!'

'Pure invention, Edwina,' declared Theo, laughing. 'And I'll keep in mind what you said about a spot of practical knowledge.'

'I'm away for a fortnight with Julius, sweetheart. Invite someone down—or up,' advised Edwina blithely.

Theo shook her head in mock reproval. 'If Mother

could hear the things you say to me, Auntie darling, she'd have a fit.'

'Rubbish. Letty may be twenty years older than me, but she has all her marbles, just the same!'

Christmas was quiet, as expected, but very enjoyable, and Theo stayed on in Cheltenham over the New Year as planned before returning to her writing. Edwina planned to travel straight back to Birmingham from her holiday and Theo had the prospect of at least ten uninterrupted days once her parents delivered her at Honeysuckle Cottage, complete with a mountain of provisions and the microwave cooker they had given her for Christmas. Edwina's present had been a video recorder she intended to share, she warned, and with it six tapes of classic Cary Grant films, since Edwina always maintained that if only she could find a man like Cary Grant she would reverse her entire outlook on matrimony on the spot.

After a week or so away from the privacy of the cottage, Theo was very glad of its silence and peace, relishing it after days spent with parents and grandparents and assorted relations, much as she loved them all. She buckled down with a will to the adventures of Ranulph and Adelise, and their stormy love-hate relationship, only breaking off at intervals for a meal or to go to bed. For the first three days she seemed driven by the need to liberate the words piled up in her brain during her period of idleness, and she scribbled until her fingers ached and her body was stiff from sitting in one position. The weather was very cold, and for warmth she took to writing downstairs in the firelit parlour, her writing block on her knee, replenishing the fire now and then with more logs, and banking it up at night with coal, to avoid having to relight it in the morning.

On the evening of the third day she slowed down a little, cooked herself a proper meal and took a long, leisurely bath afterwards, going downstairs to dry her wet hair in front of the fire while she watched one of the films. It had begun to snow during the afternoon and the wind was rising, and Theo stretched out on the sofa with a contented sigh, insulated from the wind by Edwina's double-glazing, warm and replete from her meal and the satisfaction of a good day's work behind her.

Philadelphia Story was half-way through when a loud knock on the door brought her to her feet, startled. People never came calling out this way at night, particularly in weather like this. Theo turned off the video and stood tense, waiting, then the knocking came again, louder this time and more insistent. The front door of the cottage led directly into the parlour and Theo went across to it, breathing rapidly, frankly scared.

'Who is it?' she called, as the wind howled outside, increasing her uneasiness.

'Let me in, Theodora,' a harsh voice commanded, to her mingled astonishment and relief. 'Let me in, *please*. It's James.'

CHAPTER SEVEN

WITH unsteady hands Theo fastened her sash tightly at the waist of her green wool dressing-gown, then slid back the heavy bolts and unlocked the door to let her uninvited visitor into the house.

James stamped his feet on the doorstep and came into the room, brushing snow from the shoulders of his jacket and shaking more from his hair. His eyes never left Theo's face as she closed and locked the door again, then turned to him, her fear replaced by cold, silent enquiry.

'Hello, Theodora,' he said quietly, looking very tall in the low-ceilinged room, the crown of his head almost touching the black, central beam.

'Hello, James.' How silly we sound, she thought, doing the social niceties as though this were first thing in the morning in Turnham Green instead of late at night in the wilds of Gloucestershire, with no other human being for at least a mile. At that thought her isolation struck Theo with force, and she gave an involuntary glance towards the telephone.

'You won't need the police, Theodora, I promise,' said James, interpreting her look accurately.

'I'm glad. Won't you sit down?' Theo settled herself in a small, buttoned velvet chair beside the fire, waving her visitor to the sofa. 'How did you know where to find me?'

He sat down rather wearily, his eyes still fixed on her face. 'I received a telephone call from a Miss Edwina Myers.' He smiled faintly. 'She described herself as your maiden aunt.'

'Edwina!' Theo stared at him incredulously, her lips tightening. 'And just what did Edwina see fit to tell you?'

'Merely that you were living at this address, and if I wished to contact you some time this week you'd be alone here. By which I gather your—companion is away.'

'Yes,' said Theo, with perfect truth.

'The man I saw you with before Christmas. Does—is he——?'

'No.'

There was silence while James stared sombrely at Theo, and she kept her eyes on the crackling logs. Out of the corner of her eye she saw him suddenly shiver, and jumped up. 'You're cold. Would you like some coffee?'

'If it's not too much trouble,' he said stiffly.

This was absurd, thought Theo, as she put coffee to perk and set a tray. It's past nine, there's a blizzard howling out there and yet James Hackett turns up on the doorstep without a word of warning. She was fully entitled to ask what the devil he thought he was playing at, but somehow it wasn't easy. Something occurred to her and she popped her head round the door to the parlour.

'Have you had dinner, James?'

He opened his mouth to say no and changed it to yes and Theo smiled a little. 'Perhaps you could manage a sandwich, even so?' she said, and went back to the kitchen to assemble some ham sandwiches, added some slices of her mother's excellent Christmas cake to the tray and returned to James. He sprang up to take it from her and put it down on the small oak table between them.

'Help yourself,' said Theo. 'I ate hours ago.' She waved a hand at her dressing-gown. 'Sorry for my informal appearance. I wasn't expecting company, so I washed my hair.'

'So I see.' James looked at it as he bit into a sandwich hungrily, and Theo resisted the urge to touch a hand to the untidy damp mass.

'Have you come straight from London?' she asked politely.

James nodded in silence, plainly enjoying the food.

'Rather a long journey in weather like this,' she commented. 'Do you intend driving back tonight?'

'No. I called in at the Mason's Arms in the village and booked a room for the night.' James finished off the sandwiches and made a start on the cake while Theo sipped coffee in uneasy silence, trying not to look at him. At last she could stand it no longer.

'James. Why are you here?'

He leaned back against the sofa cushions to drink his coffee, not answering immediately. His face looked pale and drawn, and the piercing blue eyes were hooded and slightly bloodshot, as though he were sleeping badly. He had left London without his necessary second shave of the day, which gave him a sinister, dangerous look Theo noted with some misgiving.

'I would have come before,' he began at last. 'Your aunt gave me your address before Christmas.'

'But your social whirl hasn't allowed the time,' said Theo tartly, then flushed as James gave her a searching look.

'I would have come before,' he repeated expressionlessly, 'but I needed to see you alone, and this was the time Miss Myers hinted would be best.'

'I see.'

'You look well, Theodora,' he said. 'As you did that day in London. Very beautiful and prosperous.'

'Borrowed plumes. The clothes were Edwina's.'

James raised his eyebrows, but made no comment. 'A few days before I saw you at Le Château,' he went on, 'I was buying a newspaper on my way into the office and noticed a paperback on one of those carousel things in the shop. The book caught my eye, as you can imagine, since it was written by someone called Theodora Grace. I bought it and read it as soon as I got home that night. I not only found the story interesting, but also the potted biography of the author on the back cover.' His eyes held hers very deliberately. 'And what's more I found the hero, Jason Harcourt, was remarkably familiar, even to the hair and eyes. But it was the name that struck me most; you let it slip one day, and I naturally assumed it was your lover. You *let* me think so, didn't you? The chap in the book was like me in a lot of ways, I found.'

So the cat was out of the bag. Theo shrugged indifferently. 'Only his worst characteristics. I had to invent his sensitivity and consideration and so on.'

The blue eyes never wavered. 'But he *was* based on me?'

'Yes. He was my safety valve. The only way I could survive my working day as that meek mouse of a secretary I was pretending to be was to pour it all out at night on paper.'

'So you worked for me by day and wrote at night?'

'Yes.'

'Not surprising you looked like death warmed up!'

'Exactly. Burning the midnight oil.'

James looked away into the fire. 'And that morning— when I came to look for you. Had you been up late writing?'

'No. Quite the opposite. I'd finished typing the book the night before, so I slept late.'

'You write well,' he said.

'You already knew that.'

'True. You were always expert at polishing up the stuff I dictated.' He gave her a twisted smile. 'These days I'm obliged to send some things back a second or third time to the present bearer of your title. She's the third since you left.'

'Third?'

'Ben Arrowsmith let me have the Robson girl for a while at first, but that was a mistake. He got her back double quick, with my blessing.'

Theo frowned at him in surprise. 'But Carol's very competent.'

James raised an eyebrow. 'She is. But she developed a propensity for working late—alone with me.'

'Ah!'

'Something you never suffered from, of course.'

'I never refused to work late when necessary!'

'But not for the sake of my bonny blue eyes, Theodora.' Those same blue eyes held a rueful smile as he said it, and involuntarily Theo responded to it.

'Who was the man I saw you lunching with?' he asked abruptly.

'Miles Hay, my editor.' She gave an embarrassed little laugh. 'Sounds very big-headed—"my editor". I mean he's one of the editorial directors at Diadem, the publishers.'

The corner of James's mouth turned down a little. 'So that was a business lunch. I only wish mine were as entertaining.'

'We were discussing my next book.'

'You're writing another one?'

'Yes. I'm half-way through.'

'Same setting?'

'No. Twelfth century this time, Crusades and so on.'

There was irony in James's look. 'And who's the model for your hero this time?'

'I don't have anyone specific. He's a product of my research, I suppose.'

'And is *he* caring and considerate?'

Theo laughed. 'No way! He's a man of his time. Any

subtlety he posseses is expended on battle strategy, not the opposite sex.' She got up to see to the fire, but James forestalled her, bending to add logs from the basket beside the hearth. As he straightened he looked around with a professional eye.

'Recently renovated, I see. Very well, too. Must have cost a pretty penny.'

Theo agreed, thinking of Edwina's loan from the bank.

James eyed her as she poured more coffee. 'This place—does it belong to—to your companion?' The word seemed to stick in his throat.

'Yes.'

'Are you here alone a lot?'

'Most of the time, really.'

His brows came together. 'It's very isolated. Do you have neighbours?'

'Only at weekends.'

'What happens if you need something suddenly, if you feel ill?'

Theo looked unconcerned. 'There's always the telephone, and my parents visit me regularly.'

James looked morose. 'They approve of the arrangement, then?'

'Yes, they do.'

There was silence after that, heavy with tension, while Theo's mind worked furiously, wild with curiosity to learn the reason for James's visit.

'How are things at the company?' she asked at last.

'Much the same as usual.'

'A lot of new projects since I left, I suppose?'

'Enough.'

'How is the Rocha do Sol venture doing?'

'Very well. All the houses sold now, and most of the holiday lets booked for this year.' James smiled sardonically. 'Why? Fancy another trip there some time?'

'Not really. I was making conversation,' she informed him tartly.

'When what you really want to know is how the hell I had the nerve to come here.'

'Not how. Why?' said Theo, facing him squarely.

His mouth compressed in a bitter line, then he shrugged. 'I would have thought the reason was obvious. I wanted to see you. The urge is nothing new, but I'd persuaded myself I'd begun to live with it until I saw you again that day. You looked so glowing and vital, and I wanted to tear you away from the man with you so much I almost burst a blood vessel. It was a shock, seeing you so unexpectedly.'

'I was somewhat taken aback myself,' said Theo colourlessly.

He gave a short laugh. 'Funny thing was I hadn't been to Le Château for ages, then Chloë got in touch and asked me to lunch to meet her husband. She got married recently. He had to leave early for another appointment—which is when I noticed you.'

So that was why James had been with Chloë. Theo digested the fact in silence.

'So I rang Cowper again,' went on James quietly. 'But he swore the Cheltenham address was all he had.'

'It's true. My parents forward everything here.'

'Does this lover of yours want to keep you in purdah, or something?'

'No. The decision was mine. It never occurred to me that Edwina would rat on me,' added Theo bitterly.

James leaned forward to look into her face. 'Why do you suppose she did?'

'She has a peculiar sense of humour.'

He sat back again. 'Seeing you again in London made me think fate was on my side. I was on the point of contacting your parents to plead my case when I heard from Miss Myers—which reinforced the feeling of kismet.'

'Kismet is nothing to do with you and me, James,' she said flatly. 'So. Now I know how you found me, but I'm still in the dark as to why. I assume you've not driven all this way on a foul night just to pay a social visit.'

James began to move about the room restlessly, picking up ornaments and putting them down, peering at the books on the shelves in the alcove alongside the fireplace. Although a shave had been overlooked he had changed his clothes, Theo noted, watching him. His cord trousers were old, and his jacket, though of expensive, supple leather, was rubbed and obviously well worn, in contrast to his cream wool shirt, which looked new and pristine against the shadowed line of his jaw. As a companion in the small room he was about as restful as a tiger, and Theo sighed.

'Can't you stop prowling, James?'

He turned and leaned against the blackened beam above the fireplace. 'Am I getting on your nerves?'

'Since you ask, yes.'

'You're worried about why I came. Don't be. You've heard it all before.' Suddenly he crouched down in front of her, grasping her hands in his as he looked urgently into her startled eyes. 'Theodora, listen to me.'

'I appear to be a captive audience,' she said tartly, and tried to take her hands away, but his fingers tightened.

'If this sort of thing is what you want I'll buy a cottage for you, anywhere you say, and you can live in it part of the time and the rest of the time in town with me. Leave this man, Theodora. I can give you anything you want, anything he does, and more. I know very well you're not indifferent to me—I can feel you trembling now.'

'That's indignation, not passion,' she flung at him. 'I don't *want* to live with you, James. I want to live here, and write in peace and lead the life here I want with—with Ranulph.'

'Ranulph!' Suddenly his eyes narrowed. 'Hold on, Jason turned out to be fictional. Could Ranulph be the same?' He shook her slightly. 'Well? Tell me!'

'No,' lied Theo spiritedly and gave him a violent shove, which rocked him off balance for a moment.

'I don't believe you.' James sprang up, agile as a cat, and returned to the bookshelves, where her writing block lay alongside a row of reference and history books. He seized it and flicked through the handwritten pages before Theo could stop him, and she stood in defiance, pushing her hair back from her mutinous face. 'Well, well,' he said with relish. 'Ranulph FitzRoy, is he? Big, redheaded fellow—quite different from Jason—and me.' His eyes met hers with a gleam Theo disliked intensely. 'Why did you lie, Theodora? Why did you let me think you had a lover—two, even? Were they a defence against me?'

'In a way. I hoped you'd back off if you thought I was involved with someone else.'

'So you always meant to leave me, once your first book was accepted?' A pulse throbbed at the corner of his mouth.

'Yes. Not as suddenly as I did, admittedly. In the end circumstances rather accelerated my departure.'

They faced each other like adversaries in front of the fire, the tension crackling between them in concert with the flames.

'I often wondered about that,' said James softly. 'Was it my lovemaking that made you run, or the mere fact of discovery?'

'A combination of both, I suppose.' Theo forced herself to meet his eyes squarely. 'Whatever it was made it impossible for me to continue working for you, particularly when you so kindly informed me you'd been conducting a little experiment.'

James smiled bitterly. 'You believed that? That I had thoughts for anything except the feel of you in my arms, the magic of having you respond to me? Then we were interrupted and you were utterly appalled and I was hurt, and said what I did to salve my own pride.' There was naked appeal in his eyes as they met hers. 'I want you, Theodora. I can't get that night out of my mind. God knows, I've tried, but I can't. I never imagined hankering after any one woman, and certainly not one who doesn't hanker after me. Yet I just can't accept the fact that you're indifferent to me, not when I think of you in my arms, and the little smothered sounds you made——'

'Shut up!' Theo glared at him in outrage. 'That was a temporary aberration on my part, James. Nothing more. So please go. I'm sorry you had a wasted journey, but I didn't ask you to come.'

'I'll be damned if it's entirely wasted!' A warning light flared in the blue eyes and Theo backed away, but the seat of her chair met the back of her knees and she sat down abruptly. James immediately pulled her up and into his arms. He tipped her head back and laid his mouth on hers with a muffled sound in his throat, as though her kiss were sustenance and he was starving. Theo stood rigid, her lips closed against him. She struggled to push him away, but James was as fit as ever, and after weeks of scribbling curled up in a chair all day long she was no match for the strength he exerted so negligently to hold her still.

In the end Theo was forced to give in and her body relaxed. At once James shifted his mouth to her hair and held her close. He drew in a long, shuddering breath and Theo leaned her cheek against the soft wool of his shirt, feeling his hand gentle on the slippery tangle of her hair. It was a long time before either of them moved.

'Let me stay,' whispered James, after a long, dreamlike interval, and Theo came to with a start.

'No.' She pushed him away firmly.

'Why not?' His taut face warned her of the iron control he was exercising over himself, but she shook her head at him scathingly.

'You honestly don't see why not, do you? Just because you want something you think you must have it.'

'Not true,' he retorted. 'I've worked for everything I have.'

'Not women.' Theo met his eyes very directly. 'Admit it, James. I'm the first one you've ever had to make the least effort to persuade.'

His eyes shuttered instantly. 'Yes. I suppose you are.'

'And why do you think that is, James?'

'I haven't the faintest idea. I thought it was because you had someone else, but now I'm stumped.'

Theo sighed. 'You may be astute and clever in the world of machines and men, James Hackett, but you can be incredibly obtuse when it comes to women.'

'One woman, apparently. You.'

'How can you expect me to drop into your arms like a ripe plum when I know only too well what a bastard you can be at times?'

'Better not let my mother hear you say that. She might take exception to the inference!'

'I meant no offence to Mrs Hackett. She has my sympathy!'

'Don't be childish, Theodora.' The old, hard glint was back in James's eyes, and the brief harmony of a few moments before vanished, like smoke up the chimney.

'What I'm trying to say,' said Theo with some attempt at patience, 'is that I'm far too well acquainted with the daytime persona of James Hackett ever to trust the smooth, off-duty version of him I knew for a brief time in Rocha do Sol.'

'My behaviour towards you when we got back was coloured by the belief that you had another man. In short,' he hit out, 'I was jealous.'

Theo nodded. 'Miles Hay said you were.'

'Did he now!' said James dangerously. 'Of course, the editor. He'd slipped my mind. Nothing fictional about Hay, as I recall.'

'You're missing the point,' she said dismissively. 'When I was dowdy and self-effacing I was invisible to you, except as someone to work like a mule because she never complained. The only feelings 'Grace' ever inspired in you were mild panic when she looked ill in case she could no longer perform her robotic function as the perfect secretary.' Theo's lip curled. 'My God, when I look back on it I can't believe I put up with all the flak you dished out! Only two things kept me at the grindstone, the thought that one day my book might be accepted, and that I was saving most of the salary I earned to finance myself for the day when I could leave to write full time. You had no compassion for Grace as a person, James. Your real interest in me dated from the moment you saw me for the first time as I really am. So it's only my physical appearance you're interested in, not the heart and brain functioning behind it.'

'That's where you're wrong,' said James instantly. 'I want all of you.'

'For how long?' she countered, folding her arms.

James looked blank. 'What do you mean?'

'A week or two. Months, perhaps?' She smiled, her voice honeyed. 'Or until death us do part?'

He went still. 'I'm not the marrying kind, Theodora——'

'No? Well don't worry,' she said kindly. 'Neither am I.'

'Then I fail to see the problem! Come and live with me——'

'And be your love—*pro tem*!'

'Let me finish,' he rapped in familiar boardroom style. 'Live part of your life with me in London and part of it in the country if you must. Write when we're apart and enjoy life with me when we're together. I could take you travelling—think of the material you could gather first-hand for your novels, the locations you could describe.'

'And when this idyll came to an end?'

'I'd provide you with a home wherever you chose, and I'd be generous, I promise.'

'You mean I'd get a lump sum for services rendered?'

'Don't try to cheapen it!'

'I don't have to try!' she flung back.

James glared at her, breathing hard. 'Don't push me too far. You know how short my fuse is better than anyone.'

'So go,' she said baldly.

'Is that all you have to say?' he demanded.

'Not by any means, but it's all I'm going to, otherwise I'll descend to insult and abuse—all the things I left unsaid during that first year with you.' Telltale colour waved flags in Theo's cheeks and her eyes burned with animosity.

James returned the look with interest. 'Something just occurred to me,' he ground out. 'Since these lovers of yours are fictional, just exactly who *does* foot the bill for this expensive little nest? Your suave editor?'

Theo was sorely tempted to say yes, but she shook her head. 'It belongs to Edwina. The aunt who kindly informed you where I was.'

'And just why did she do that, do you suppose?'

'I don't know. It's something I intend to take up with her at the first opportunity.'

James cast a meaning look towards the narrow stairway that led straight from the room to the floor above. 'Perhaps she felt you needed—company.'

Suddenly a log fell in the fireplace and Theo, nerves stretched to breaking point, let out a gasp of fright and James lunged, catching her in his arms to kiss her with a hunger sharpened by the acrimony between them. This time, almost from the start, Theo realised resistance was useless. The man holding her had passed beyond the limit of his own control, and suddenly she yielded to him, all the fight in her consumed in the flame burning inside James like a forest fire. She gave up, letting his mouth draw a fevered response from her own while his hands travelled over her body in desperate need of contact with her skin. They stripped her of the dressing-gown and slid beneath the heavy satin of her pyjamas, and she shook at their touch, shook at the fevered, undreamed-of things he whispered in her ears as he lowered her to the sofa cushions, holding her there by means of one long leg thrown over hers as he tore off his jacket and shirt and came down to hold her in an embrace that blocked out the world.

James raised his head at one point and looked down at her, stern and austere in the extremity of the desire that gripped him. 'I want you, Theodora,' he said hoarsely. 'If you never let me near you again so be it, but, God help me, if I don't have you now, I'll go mad.'

Theo had given up all thoughts of opposition by that stage and closed her eyes and let herself drown in his urgency, surfacing briefly when he drew her down to the hearthrug and spent long moments in just looking at her body in the firelight. Then his mouth came down on hers and his clever hands drew a wild response from her body, teasing it to a pinnacle of quivering tension that tautened and threatened to snap like an overtuned violin string. His body found hers and the tension broke and she cried out in relief, only to find a different tension building inside her with every thrust of the big powerful body that was taking her higher and higher and further and further towards some peak of rapture just beyond her reach. Frantically she clung to him, her nails digging into the smooth brown skin of his shoulders, racked with a frenzy of longing for the unknown summit. Then she reached it and gave a harsh, choked cry and she was free-falling through space and it was over and she was back to earth.

Theo lay beneath the weight of James's body, unable to move. His dishevelled black hair lay against her face, his head heavy on her shoulder, and his arms held her like iron bands. What, she thought with detachment, should she do now? If James had any sense of occasion he ought to be muttering words of fevered apology into her ears instead of pinning her down to the rug, which, now she was more in a position to notice, was distinctly scratchy to her bare skin.

James stirred after a while. 'I don't know what to say,' he muttered indistinctly.

Theo frowned, disappointed. 'Just now you had plenty to say,' she pointed out, and felt him wince. 'Things I'd never heard before, I might add.'

'Unfair.'

'Not in the least. All's fair in love and war. And what happened just now came more or less into both categories, wouldn't you say?'

James raised his head and looked at her. 'You're very calm.'

Theo thought it over. 'Not calm. Exhausted.'

'I thought you'd be attacking me with the poker by now.'

'Not much point at this stage. I should have done it earlier on.' She smiled at him politely. 'Would you get up now, please? I can't breathe.'

James leapt to his feet and turned his back on her as he pulled on his clothes in silence. With an effort Theo heaved herself up and retrieved her dressing-gown. She wrapped herself up in it, yawning, and, with a word of apology, went upstairs to the bathroom. The face in the mirror was very flushed and heavy-eyed, with noticeably swollen lips. Not much doubt what you've been up to, she informed it, splashed it with cold water and went downstairs. James was standing in front of the newly made-up fire, fully dressed. His hair was untidy, but otherwise he looked much the same as usual, to her resentment. As she went down the last few steps into the room James eyed her warily.

'So what happens now, Theodora?'

She shrugged. 'Nothing. You go down to the Mason's Arms for the night, then back to London in the morning, and life goes on as usual.'

'As usual,' he repeated without inflexion.

'Yes.'

He stared at her blankly. 'You mean we pretend that tonight never happened?'

Theo smiled faintly. 'A trifle difficult to do that. But it did, and that's that. You came to see me and did what you really came to do, I assume. I was a loose end, wasn't I, James? Well, now I've been tidied up and you can forget about me.'

'Is that what you think?' he demanded harshly.

'Yes. I do.'

'I came here to persuade you to share my life, Theodora,' he said tightly. 'Not something I've ever asked any woman before.'

'Oh, come on!' she protested. 'You were living with Chloë Masson not so long ago, and I'm sure she wasn't the first.'

'With the others,' James said very deliberately, 'there was no persuasion involved.'

'Oh, I see.' Theo shrugged. 'Well, I'm afraid that as far as I'm concerned, as I told you before, there's no place for you in my life. I'm sorry, but you take up too much room—in every way.'

James rubbed his eyes wearily. 'You're as obstinate as a mule.'

'I just *love* your way with words!'

'You appeared pleased with those I used earlier.'

That was hitting below the belt. Theo gave him a cold stare. 'I hardly heard what you were saying.'

'So I noticed. You seemed more concerned with what I was doing.' His smile was gentle, at variance with his words, which reached their target with painful precision.

'You play dirty, James,' she said bitterly.

'Only when I have to,' he said swiftly, and moved nearer. 'What we just experienced was in no way ordinary, Theodora. I have never experienced anything remotely like it before. Take my word for it—you and I are highly compatible.'

'It was the way it was because I'd been opposing you, because we'd been quarrelling and our emotions were abnormally heightened—oh, lots of reasons.' Theo looked away, biting her lip. 'If we lived together you'd very soon become used to me, take me for granted. It probably wouldn't be like tonight ever again.'

'My God—you're supposed to be a romantic novelist,' he said angrily. 'Is that the way you see life with a man?'

'I'm a woman who writes romantic fiction,' Theo corrected. 'It doesn't prevent me from seeing things the way they are. Even when I wore glasses to work they were never rose-tinted, James. I saw you very clearly.'

'So that's it, then.' James went to the door, turning to look at her after he unlocked it. 'I suppose I should apologise for making love to you, but since it was something we both enjoyed to the full it seems pointless. I haven't changed my mind, Theodora. I still want you to come to me. On any terms.'

'Except marriage, of course!'

'Except marriage. I don't believe in it. If it's any consolation,' he added, 'you're the only woman I've ever met I'd want to marry me if I did.'

Theo's eyes dropped before the burn in his. 'How very flattering, James.'

'No flattery—it's the truth. But as an eye-witness to my own parents' marriage I intend to avoid the same monumental mistake.' He crossed to Theo swiftly and bent to raise her face to his. 'But you can have anything else you want.'

'I don't want anything from you, James.'

'Then there's nothing more to say,' he said quietly and pulled her into his arms, kissing her with a controlled longing that left them both shaking as he thrust her from him and wrenched the door open on the white, howling world outside.

'Drive carefully,' said Theo unsteadily.

James smiled bleakly. 'It's not far to the village. Shut the door and let me hear you lock and bolt it before I leave.'

Theo did as he said, then parted the curtains at the window to watch his tall figure out of sight. She heard him start the car and winced as the wheels spun before getting a grip on the snow-coated ruts of the lane, then there was a roar as the powerful engine took off and seconds later the night was quiet except for the mournful sound of the wind.

CHAPTER EIGHT

'DON'T try and get round me with presents!' warned Theo, when Edwina arrived for her first weekend after the skiing trip.

Edwina's dark eyes widened innocently. 'Why? What *have* I done? Am I to be sent down without a fair trial?'

Theo brought in the casserole she'd prepared for dinner and dumped it on the small table laid for two near the fire. 'Thank you for the perfume, Auntie darling, and the chocolate bears, and I'm *so* glad you had a lovely time, but why on earth did you let James Hackett know where to find me?'

'Oh, that.' Edwina helped herself, sniffing ecstatically. 'God, I'm hungry.'

'Yes. That!' Theo gave her aunt a baleful look.

'So he came.'

'Yes.'

'And saw and conquered?' Edwina nodded as she met the incensed eyes of her niece. 'Yes, I can see he did.'

It was impossible to stay cross with Edwina for long. Against her will Theo began to laugh and Edwina smiled approvingly, and proceeded to extract the details with professional skill.

'You're the end,' declared Theo eventually. 'Not only do you stage manage James's visit, but you expect a blow-by-blow account of the entire occasion.'

'Be fair,' Edwina protested. 'All I did was give him the address. I wasn't to know whether he'd act on it, was I? Nevertheless, I'm glad he did. I was convinced you were in need of a spot of male diversion.'

Theo shook her head in despair, and asked questions

130

in turn, giggling at Edwina's verdict on her companion, who had been more concerned with the *après* bit than the skiing.

'Left to Julius I'd never have seen a ski-slope,' said Edwina ruefully. 'And what's more, when he told me he was separated from his wife it turned out to be more in body than in spirit. He had an off-putting little habit of muttering her name in his sleep, so I crossed him off the list. How about you though, what did this James of yours give as the reason for his visit—apart from the obvious, I mean?'

Theo gave an edited account of his proposition, which brought Edwina upright in her chair to stare at her niece, agog to know what her answer had been.

'The same as before. Nothing doing.' Theo smiled cheerfully and refused to talk about it any more, and Edwina obligingly returned to the more hilarious incidents of her own holiday.

Progress on the new novel was going along at a fair rate, to Theo's relief. Surprisingly, the visit from James had made no difference to her concentration. Even his lovemaking had been put to good use. Theo felt a definite pang of guilt at her cold-blooded attitude, but nevertheless their encounter provided much first-hand material for the clashes between Ranulph and his rebellious bride. Certain subtle details of their frantic interchange had been of enormous help, in fact, since her own imagination could never have come up with some of the nuances of seduction she had experienced at James's skilful, experienced hands.

But James Hackett was far too unsettling a man to have around the house, particularly a small cottage like Edwina's. For days afterwards the place had seemed full of him; even the sound of the telephone had made her tense and wary until the voice on the other end proved to be her mother or Edwina.

From James there was silence, and as time went on Theo relaxed, confident that he had finally accepted defeat. Then one morning a parcel arrived, containing a rare and expensive book on the twelfth-century struggle for power between Stephen and Matilda. Enclosed with it was a note. 'Thought this might come in handy. J.' Theo stared at the familiar handwriting and then at the book, not daring to do more than glance through it until her day's stint at her novel was over. Later that night she curled up on the sofa with her supper tray beside her and gave herself up to the intricacies of court intrigue and politics until it was time to go to bed. She lay awake longer than usual, wondering how to respond to the gift. It seemed petty and hurtful to return it. Besides, the book was a rich source of information. She didn't want to send it back.

After breakfast next morning Theo wrote a polite, appreciative little note of thanks and sent it to the Turnham Green offices. A few days later another parcel came, this time containing a beautifully bound set of Jane Austen. Theo stared at the tooled leather and gold leaf of the bindings and bit her lip. 'You may fancy writing a book on her period some time' said the note. This time it was signed 'James'. James, it seemed, was playing a devious game. Not for Theo the flowers he casually gave his other women, apparently. For herself it was literature. Very clever, she thought with a smile.

'Where did those come from?' demanded Edwina on her next visit.

'Guess.'

'James?' Edwina nodded sagely. 'Very subtle!'

'Not his usual style,' said Theo morosely. 'It was part of my job to send flowers to the Hackett amours, buy presents for them even, but never books.'

'He's determined to have his evil way with you, darling!'

'Edwina, he's already had it. Once. And that's it. He can send presents until the cows come home, but I'm not moving in with him.'

Edwina looked irritatingly unconvinced, and Theo spent most of the weekend trying to convince her that James Hackett was wasting his time. They were still arguing over coffee on Sunday morning, when a knock on the cottage door brought Theo to her feet, tense as a drawn bow.

'If that's him,' she said threateningly, and stalked across the room to throw open the door. Her face went blank with surprise. Miles Hay stood on the doorstep, his eyes dancing.

'Hello, Theo,' he said, smiling. 'I took you at your word and just dropped in. Have I come at an awkward moment?'

'No—no, of course not,' she assured him earnestly. 'Do come in, please. It's lovely to see you.' As Theo drew him into the room Edwina peeped round the parlour door to see who it was. 'Come in and meet my aunt,' added Theo.

Edwina strolled into the room, every gleaming bronze hair in place. She was wearing the gold shirt and leather skirt once lent to Theo and Miles Hay literally stopped in his tracks. Edwina held out her hand, smiling her dazzling smile.

'How do you do? I'm Edwina Myers.'

'Miles Hay,' he responded absently, taking the hand in his. 'I know it sounds a bit hackneyed, but I feel as if we've met before.'

'You've met the clothes,' said Theo, grinning. 'I was wearing them the day I lunched with you in London.'

'Oh, darling, how awful!' Edwina said ruefully, and gently removed her hand from Miles's clasp. 'So you're Theo's editor,' she said with interest. 'She was afraid you were someone else.'

The bemused look faded from Miles's face. 'I'm relieved to hear it. She looked poised for attack when she opened the door.'

Theo laughed, colouring a little, and went to make fresh coffee while Edwina entertained their unexpected visitor. Alone, she chuckled at the thought of Edwina in the now famous skirt and shirt, not at all put out that her own outfit consisted of elderly jeans and an oversized, green, jersey, since she felt surprisingly comfortable with Miles Hay, despite their short acquaintance.

Edwina appeared to feel the same way, Theo discovered, when she rejoined the other two. They were chatting away with the ease of old friends rather than people just introduced, and Edwina looked up with a pleased smile as Theo put the coffee tray down in front of her.

'Miles has invited us to lunch, darling—isn't that lovely?'

'That's very civil of you, Miles!' Theo smiled her appreciation and handed him a cup of coffee.

'I've been staying with friends in Chipping Campden and decided to take you up on your invitation since I was in the neighbourhood.' He included them both in his smile. 'Quite a way off the beaten track here, aren't you?'

'Perfect for weekends,' Edwina assured him, 'not to mention budding novelists.'

Miles nodded. 'How's the book coming along, Theo?'

'Rather well. A few stops now and then for reference purposes, but generally speaking I'm fairly satisfied.'

'Good. *The Fettered Heart* is selling well, you'll be pleased to hear.'

Edwina sighed happily. 'How marvellous! Isn't she a clever girl?'

'Takes after her aunt, perhaps?' Miles slanted a

laughing look in Edwina's direction, and Theo watched, fascinated, as rare colour rose in her aunt's face in response to the compliment.

Over lunch at the Mason's Arms in the village it was quite plain to Theo that Edwina found Miles Hay very attractive indeed, also that she was trying very hard not to let it show too much, since it was Theo he'd come to see. Miles, on the other hand, while discussing Theo's new novel at length, nevertheless managed to bring Edwina into the conversation the whole time, never letting her feel excluded. After lunch he drove them both back to Honeysuckle Cottage, lingered for an hour, then took his leave with graceful thanks for his welcome.

After seeing him to his car Theo went into the cottage to find Edwina staring abstractedly into the fire, the Sunday papers unopened beside her on the sofa.

'Well?' demanded Theo. 'Did you like him?'

Edwina turned blank eyes on her. 'Miles?'

'Yes. Miles.'

'He's a charmer. Tell me, Theo, didn't he remind you of Cary Grant?'

Theo swallowed hard on an involuntary giggle. The slimly built Miles, with his fair hair and lazy eyes, bore as much resemblance to the dark, staccato sophistication of Cary Grant as she herself did to Marilyn Monroe in her opinion, but she kept from saying so. 'I told you he was nice,' she said instead.

Edwina's face went carefully blank. 'Is he the reason why you won't do what James Hackett wants, Theo?'

Comprehension dawned. 'No, Edwina, he's not. I like him a lot, and feel very relaxed and at ease with him— none of which remotely applies to James. But that's all. I'm lucky to have such a sympathetic editor, but as far as the rest is concerned he's all yours.'

'Theo!' Edwina looked very put out. 'It was *you* he came to see.'

'And couldn't believe his luck when he found you were here as well! Besides,' added Theo teasingly, 'he's more your age group then mine, old dear.'

'Horrible child!' Edwina looked relieved, none the less, then gave her niece one of her rapier-like smiles. 'And how old is James Hackett, may I ask?'

'No you may not,' said Theo crossly, aware that James was only a couple of years younger than Miles Hay.

'Is he married?' asked Edwina pensively.

'Who?'

'Miles, of course.'

'Divorced.'

'Oh, God—another one!'

'He gave me the impression at lunch that day that it's a perfectly amicable arrangement. Wife remarried, no children to cause friction.'

'Oh.'

'So the field's free, Edwina,' said Theo gently.

For once Edwina Myers lacked the air of burnished assurance she normally wore with such aplomb. She gave Theo a troubled look. 'How do I know he's interested?'

Theo began to laugh helplessly, utterly amazed by her aunt's question. 'If he isn't he's giving the best impersonation of a smitten man I've ever seen!'

'Like James, you mean!'

'No, not like James.' Theo's smile faded. 'James is like the cat that can't catch the mouse, and I have a nasty feeling that these thoughtful presents are mere bait to put me off guard so he can pounce.'

When the next present arrived it came as a real surprise. It came, not in a parcel through the post, but curled up in a basket fast asleep, borne in the arms of a smiling girl who introduced herself as a kennelmaid for a well-known breeder of golden retrievers. Theo stared open-mouthed at the bundle of creamy-gold fur and accepted the basket, along with a list of instructions, a carton of food, a couple of feeding bowls, a collar and a leash.

'I'm instructed to say that this is something you've always wanted,' said the girl carefully, 'and that you need a guard dog in such an out-of-the-way place. A Mr James Hackett is the donor.'

Theo nodded, resigned. 'Yes. I'm sure he is.'

Left alone with the puppy, she stared at it helplessly. True, she always had wanted a dog. Whether Edwina would be so charmed at a canine addition to Honeysuckle Cottage it was hard to say. The girl from the kennels had assured Theo the dog was house-trained and past the chewing stage, but his new owner felt no confidence on either point. She bit her lip—she should have sent the animal straight back, of course.

Guard dog indeed! Still out for the count from the journey, the puppy gave a muted whimper in his sleep and Theo stroked the satiny fur gently, making instinctive soothing noises, then went back to her writing, keeping an eye on the basket from time to time. The Lady Adelise was up to her ears in rallying her household as they prepared to defend the castle from attack in the absence of Ranulph, when a slight stirring from the basket alerted Theo. She knelt down beside it as the puppy yawned widely and opened bewildered, velvet-brown eyes on his new mistress, and began to whimper. Theo's heart was wrung, and she cradled the warm little body in her arms protectively, then put him down, buckled on the new collar and attached the leash.

'Better go for a stroll,' she informed the puppy, who evidently thought the idea splendid, as he explored every bush in the back garden and lifted an unsteady leg against most of them. Indoors again Theo filled the

larger plastic bowl from one of the tins, put water in the
smaller one, and the little dog ate with enthusiasm,
drank a little, had another stagger round the garden and
then suffered itself to be cuddled into the basket again
where it promptly went to sleep.

Theo's parents paid her a visit that evening, and were
very surprised to meet the new resident of Honeysuckle
Cottage.

'A dog?' exclaimed Letty Grace, smartly removing
one of her suede boots from the puppy's attention.

'Very sensible,' said Hugh Grace in approval and
tickled the ecstatic dog in exactly the right place behind
its ear.

'That's what I thought,' said Theo firmly, finding it
quite impossible to explain that the puppy was a present
from James Hackett.

'I know you always yearned for one,' admitted Mrs
Grace with a twinkle. 'And I would never allow it
because I was sure I'd be the one left with the walkies
and the puddles on the carpet.' She raised an enquiring
eyebrow. 'How does Edwina feel about puddles and so
on?'

Theo was secretly very worried indeed about
Edwina's reaction, but made vague noises of assurance—and a mental note to ring her aunt the moment
her parents left. They stayed quite late, Theo's father
utterly captivated by the dog, which he took out for
several sorties into the garden during the course of the
evening.

'He's a very sweet little dog,' conceded Mrs Grace
when they were ready to go. 'Have you thought of a
name for him?'

'I thought Jason—after my first hero,' said Theo, and
her parents laughed and pronounced it a very suitable
choice.

It was late before Edwina answered her telephone,

and before Theo could get a word in went on and on like a teenager in the throes of her first romance because Miles Hay had rung her shortly before.

'How did he know my number, do you think?' she asked Theo.

'Because he rang me first and asked for it,' her niece informed her with some relish.

'Oh dear! Did you mind?'

'No, I did not mind——' but before Theo could say another word Edwina was off again. Miles had to be in Birmingham next day apparently, and had asked her to dinner.

'Fantastic,' Theo got in at last. 'Edwina, do shut up for a moment and listen.'

'Yes,' said Edwina, suddenly crisp and attentive. 'What is it? Something wrong? James again?'

'In a way. He's sent me another present.'

There was silence on the line for a second or two before Edwina said slowly. 'I've just noticed the time. It must be something out of the ordinary for you to ring me at this time of night.'

Theo took in a deep breath and told her about Jason, who, adorable and utterly irresistible though he might be, was, nevertheless, a dog.

'Goodness,' responded Edwina in awe. 'He *is* a clever beast!'

'Jason?'

'No, idiot. James. He seems extremely knowledgeable about all your little weaknesses, doesn't he?'

Even at the other end of a telephone line Theo went bright scarlet at the picture Edwina's words conjured in her mind. 'You haven't said whether you mind a dog at the cottage,' she said with difficulty.

'Don't let him chew the hearth rug—it's a prayer mat and valuable, and if possible make him sleep downstairs, but otherwise I think a dog's not a bad idea. Company for you.'

Weak with relief, Theo thanked her aunt and put down the telephone to inform Jason that the landlady approved of him. The instructions about the hearth rug were superfluous. It was already rolled up and stowed in the cupboard under the stairs out of harm's way, but Theo's face grew warm again as she remembered the use to which it had been put during James's visit. When Jason was installed in his basket, and the basket placed firmly on the tiled floor of the kitchen, Theo went to bed, her heart rent by pitiful cries from Jason, who shrieked his anguish for some time before he wore himself out.

Theo set her alarm to ring earlier than usual for the puppy's sake, and gave much thought to her response to James's latest present. It would seem, unless she was placing too much significance on the gifts, that James was bent on wooing her into accepting his proposal. Proposition, she amended hastily. And he was so clever about it all, too. He had a retentive memory. She had only let the name Jason slip once, yet he had instantly stored it for future reference, as he had with her mention of wanting a dog as a child. One needed care when talking to James. Not, of course, that she would be talking to James again. She had told him to go and he'd gone, but he seemed determined to keep his memory fresh in her mind by sending her books—and now Jason.

Next morning, on impulse, she decided to thank James in person and put a call through to Hackett Construction, asking to speak to the managing director. He was in a meeting, she was informed, but if she cared to leave a name, number and message, Mr Hackett would return the call. Already regretting her impulse, Theo declined, assuring the feminine voice that it was unimportant, and rang off.

Jason's advent slowed Theo's progress on her novel. He was a bright, affectionate little dog, and from the first moment he opened his eyes on Theo's face made it crystal clear he regarded her as his mother. Unless he was actually sleeping, which was often enough admittedly, he demanded attention, wanting to be cuddled and played with. An old tennis ball proved a distraction for a while, but Jason soon tired of it and Theo gave in and took him for a long walk along the footpath leading over the fields towards Bedington. By the time they got back Jason was tired out and slept for several hours while Adelise and her household strove to maintain the castle's defences against the onslaught of Guerain de St Evrier and his evil desire to seize Ranulph FitzRoy's castle and bed its chatclaine. At the height of the attack Jason woke up, so once more it was down with the pencil and on with the wellingtons so the puppy could relieve his feelings in the sodden garden. Fortunately Jason was not at all keen on the sleet-filled rain, and quite amenable to returning indoors for his lunch. Theo ate at the same time, then gave Jason a lecture on procedure, telling him that since one day he would be a large dog he could not sleep on the sofa, nor on her lap, and had to remain in the kitchen in his basket at night while his mistress went upstairs to bed.

'I am a person,' she informed him firmly. 'You are a dog. So keep it in mind.'

Jason sat looking up at her, head cocked adorably on one side, reducing Theo secretly to a sentimental mush, but she controlled the urge to pick him up and hug him. Luckily he was very taken with the fire when she lit it. The flames seemed to mesmerise him and he sat, staring into it, fascinated, until gradually he subsided into a little heap and went to sleep, letting Theo get on with her story.

Later that evening, while Theo and Jason were

enjoying a film curled up together in front of the fire, the telephone rang.

'Hello,' answered Theo absently, her eyes still on the television screen.

'Hello, Theodora.'

She breathed in sharply at the sound of the hard, assured voice. 'Who is this?' she asked sweetly.

'The big bad wolf, Red Riding Hood—as you well know.'

'Hello, James,' she said resigned.

'You rang me today, I think, so I'm returning the call.'

Theo's eyes narrowed to fierce, angry slits and she crossed the fingers of her free hand. 'That's very kind of you, but it wasn't me,' she lied.

'Naughty, naughty. Fibs, Theodora. Since the lady refused to give her name it must have been you. Any other, er, friend of mine would have been only too keen for me to know who rang.'

His logic affected her like a brush down with a bunch of nettles. 'Why,' she said with deliberation, 'should you imagine I would want to ring you?'

'To thank me for my present, perhaps. I checked that it had been delivered. Or perhaps you were seized with the urge to talk to me.'

'Wrong on both counts. I wrote you the usual note.' Which was the truth. Jason had accompanied her to the post-box at the end of the lane earlier on.

'Ah, well,' he sighed. 'I can dream, can't I? I do, you know. Then I wake up sweating, and need a cold shower before I can sleep again—don't hang up!'

Theo stared at the receiver stonily. How had he known she was about to bang it back on the cradle? she wondered.

'Tell me,' went on James, 'how did you like the puppy?'

'The guard dog, you mean.'

'He'll soon grow. And I think you need a dog all alone in that cottage, miles from anywhere.'

'You're making me nervous.'

'Nonsense. You, Theodora? Nervous?'

'It's not impossible, you know. I'm just as prone to nerves as any other female.'

'You surprise me. I always picture you equal to anything——'

Theo cut him short by thanking him for the dog. 'It was a very expensive present, and quite impossible to return, of course.'

'You said you'd always wanted one.'

'I know. Thank you.' Theo relented and laughed a little. 'Actually, he's utterly irresistible, but terribly demanding.'

'Just like me,' said James promptly.

'Now look here, James,' she said hotly. 'Since we *are* talking, I must ask you to stop sending me things. It won't do any good.'

'What can you mean?' he said mockingly.

'I won't change my mind.'

'About what?'

'You know very well,' she said between her teeth.

'Haven't the foggiest, but I'm glad you like the puppy. What have you called him?'

'Jason.'

'Ah! After your hero.'

'Not really.' Theo crossed her fingers again. 'His coat made me think of golden fleece.'

'Very classical. Even my education ran to a spot of Greek myth.'

'You're a snob. Inverted variety.'

'How unpleasant you are to me, Theodora!'

'I was taught how by a master.'

There was silence for a moment, then James said

quietly. 'You win, Theodora. I'll let you have the last word. Goodnight.'

'Goodnight.' Theo put down the telephone feeling deflated, and resumed her former place beside Jason, who licked her energetically until she put a stop to it. 'Enough, Jason, enough. Now, tell me what happened while I was away.'

Theo was back to her habit of jumping out of her skin every time the telephone rang for a while after James's call, but gradually got over it as the effort of training Jason took up all her free time. She informed her mother that trips to Cheltenham were out for the time being until Jason was foolproof in the puddle department. He was already very good, but Theo considered a change of environment inadvisable at this stage. Edwina took one look at Jason and fell madly in love, proving to be the one Theo was obliged to discipline in the matter of bedtime arrangements and forbidden titbits.

'I've explained to him that he's a dog,' said Theo firmly. 'Don't confuse him, please.'

Edwina sighed and tickled Jason's tummy. 'But he's so cuddly and cute.'

'For Pete's sake, Edwina, don't be so yucky. Remember, you're only here at weekends. It's good old Theo who's here most of the time, and good old Theo's trying to write a novel as well as train a dog.'

'Don't blame me, love. Blame James. He gave him to you.' Edwina sat up, looking at Theo searchingly. 'Been in touch, has he?'

How did she know? fumed Theo in secret. Did it stand out all over her? 'He rang,' she admitted briefly.

'And?'

'And nothing. I said thank you and told him to stop sending me things. Anyway, how about you? Enjoy you dinner with Miles?'

Edwina had. Very much, she confessed, and looked a

trifle sheepish. In her opinion she was getting on a bit to feel so dewy-eyed about a man. To reach the ripe old age of thirty-seven without falling in love was one thing, but then to do it twice in one week hinted at a deterioration in her mental powers!

'*Twice?*'

Edwina grinned. 'First Miles—now Jason. Who next, I wonder!'

'Perhaps you should meet James Hackett!'

'No. I don't think he's my type, somehow, from what you've told me. And, dear niece, Auntie has no intention of poaching on your preserves a second time.'

'If you're referring to Miles you're not guilty, and as far as James is concerned, neither am I.'

'I do wish I could believe that,' said Edwina pensively, then ducked to dodge the cushion Theo aimed at her.

CHAPTER NINE

As time went on Theo became convinced that the puppy had been a parting gift, since nothing more came in the days and weeks that followed. She decided she was relieved. James had finally seen sense. Life was busy and peaceful and only very slightly dull. Nevertheless she was more than pleased to take a break with her mother and father when Edwina announced rather tentatively that Miles Hay had been invited for the weekend. There was absolutely no need for Theo to remove herself, Edwina said emphatically, but Theo was only too glad to leave the field clear for her aunt.

'But I'm leaving Jason as chaperon,' she warned. 'He's more or less trained now, but strange surroundings might unsettle him, and God help us all if there was a puddle—or worse—on Mother's new carpet!'

It was late on Sunday evening by the time Hugh Grace had driven Theo back to the cottage and Edwina was on her way to Birmingham. Miles had left after lunch, and one look at the starry-eyed Edwina had been enough to learn that the weekend had been an unqualified success. Theo threw a couple of cushions on the floor and lay reading, the puppy cuddled blissfully against her. She felt rather flat, even though Jason had been gratifyingly demonstrative about how much he'd missed her, and now she was back in the cottage she felt oddly restless.

She jumped up to take Jason into the garden, shivering a little in the raw February night as the puppy took his time over his investigation of the undergrowth.

Eventually she rounded him up and he dashed into the house ahead of her, setting up a sudden staccato barking once he was inside. Theo tore into the house and came to a sudden halt, her heart in her mouth as she saw James crouched near the door, his long fingers tickling the puppy.

'Good evening,' said Theo, her heart thudding. 'How——?'

'The door was unlocked, Theodora.' James rose slowly to his feet, his eyes moving hungrily over her.

'Was it? How careless of me. Well—this is an unexpected pleasure. Won't you sit down?' Theo schooled her face to some sort of civility, secretly appalled at just how much pleasure it actually gave her to see James again.

'I was in the neighbourhood and thought I'd drop in to see how you and your guard dog are getting along.' He grinned as Jason seized one of his shoelaces between his teeth and began tugging. 'I hope he's not too much of a handful.'

'No. He's getting quite obedient, in fact.' To demonstrate Theo clicked her fingers and said sharply, 'Sit, Jason!'

The little dog complied, to her relief, looking at her with such a smug air of conceit James laughed, regarding Theo with respect.

'I'm impressed!'

'He's great company.' Theo looked away, feeling oddly shy.

'And you get lonely?'

'Sometimes.'

'I thought your life was so full you had no time to feel lonely.'

Theo looked up sharply, but there was no malice in the blue eyes. 'Everyone gets lonely now and then, surely!' She recalled herself hurriedly. 'May I offer you coffee, or a drink?'

'Thank you. Whatever's easiest.'

The kitchen cupboard, where Edwina kept wine occasionally, boasted a half-full bottle of single malt whisky and another of gin. Theo raised her eyebrows. In Miles's honour, presumably. She poured whisky into a tumbler, added a dash of gin to a glass of orange juice for herself, and went back to the parlour.

'Single malt,' she announced, as she handed the glass to James. 'I didn't think you'd want water in it—or ice.'

'Very proper, Theodora, a sin to dilute it.' James raised his glass. 'To you. It seems a very long time since I saw you last.' His eyes kindled as they met hers, and Theo felt her face go hot, left in no doubt that he was thinking of their last meeting, and one aspect of it in particular. James glanced involuntarily towards the hearthrug and frowned. 'What happened to the rug?'

'I put it away to protect it from Jason. Edwina informs me it's a prayer mat and valuable,' said Theo, looking away.

'A prayer mat,' he repeated, and took a large swallow of whisky.

There was silence for a while, broken only by Jason's snores, then both Theo and James spoke together and broke off.

'I'm sorry, Theodora—what were you saying?' he asked quickly.

'Nothing, really. I just wondered where you were today, that's all.'

'Cardiff.'

'Cardiff!' She stared at him. 'That's not exactly in the neighbourhood.'

'No, I suppose not. I was visiting my mother over the

weekend and on the way back decided to make a detour to see you.'

'Rather a long way round to London!'

'Yes.' James stared into his glass and Theo examined his averted profile unobserved. The grey streaks were more plentiful in his dark hair, and his face looked drawn and tired.

'Life busy at Hackett Construction?' she asked.

'Yes. Gratifyingly so.' James turned to meet her eyes. 'And you, Theodora? Are you busy too?'

'Very. I've almost finished writing my book. I'll be able to make a start on typing it soon.'

'Why don't you type it first off?'

'I can't. It won't come that way for some reason. I have to see it on the page as I scribble or it just doesn't happen.'

'But you enjoy writing.' It was a statement, not a question.

'Yes, James. Very much.'

'So you haven't changed your mind?'

'About what?'

James tossed down the last of his whisky and abruptly the preliminaries were over.

'Don't fence with me, Theodora,' he said bluntly. 'We both know why I'm here. Because I bloody well couldn't stay away any longer. I'm like a schoolboy with his first crush. All I can think about is you. There, in front of the fire. Your skin burning mine as we made love. The thought of it keeps me awake at night, visits me suddenly in the middle of a meeting when my mind should be fully occupied with other things.' His eyes fastened on hers and she stared back helplessly, her mouth drying as the bitter, self-derisory voice went on. 'I want you, Theodora, more than any other woman I've ever known.'

Her mouth set mutinously. 'Because I say no, as I said before, rather than for any particular quality I possess.'

'Wrong,' he contradicted emphatically. 'I came here tonight with one purpose in mind—no, not that,' as Theo's eyes went involuntarily to the hearth. 'I came to try to persuade you one more time.'

'To come and live with you?'

James nodded, making no attempt to touch her. 'Yes. You can make the terms. I'll settle for anything you say. Just weekends if that's the way you want it.'

'A sort of part-time love affair,' she said cuttingly, 'not that "love" is particularly apposite in this instance.'

There was cynical honesty in his eyes as he shrugged in answer. 'I don't know much about love, except what I feel for my mother. When it comes to the other variety I find it hard to believe in such an emotion as anything but ephemeral. I only know that whatever it is I feel for you is stronger and more consuming than anything I've ever felt before.'

'Are you quite sure it's not my novelty that attracts you most, James?'

'Novelty?'

'Yes. Because I won't give in. Not physically, of course. I can't deny that on that score you won hands down. But otherwise I don't intend to let you possess me.'

'Otherwise?' he repeated, his eyes narrowing.

'On a higher level,' said Theo shortly. 'Like heart and mind and so on. My body may have given in once, I know, but the rest of me didn't.'

James stood up and pulled her from her chair, staring down into her rebellious eyes. 'If your body gave in once, perhaps it could again.'

Theo shook her head and tried to pull away, and suddenly Jason woke up and began to bark and jump up, obviously of the opinion the game was open to everyone. The tension in James's body slackened, and he relinquished his hold on Theo's arms. There was a wry look on his face as he bent to soothe the dog.

'Hey, you, it wasn't part of my plan for you to defend her from me, you know.'

Theo relaxed a little. 'He's only doing his duty.'

James straightened and faced her, his eyes expressionless. 'So the answer's no, Theodora?'

Theo was no longer as certain of this as she would have liked. 'I just want to write, James,' she said evasively.

'While I just want you.'

Colour flooded her face and she looked down, away from the searching blue eyes that seemed to see right into her brain. 'Don't, James.'

He moved closer and put a finger under her chin, lifting her face so that she was forced to look at him. 'One day I'll win, I promise you.'

She shook her head. 'I shouldn't count on it.'

Swiftly James bent his head and kissed her, holding her lightly by the shoulders. Instantly a tremor ran through them both, and with a groan James held her closer, his lips moving on hers, and the dog sat watching them, some instinct telling him this was no longer a game. At last James lifted his head, his face pale as he stared into Theo's dazed eyes. 'For God's sake, *why*, darling? Why won't you come to me?'

'You'll take me over,' she said desperately. 'I'd never have a life of my own. I know you too well.'

The familiar pulse throbbed at a corner of his mouth as he looked down at her, then at last James rubbed a hand wearily over his eyes and turned away. 'All right,' he said in a muffled voice. 'I'll go. I was a fool to come.' He laughed mirthlessly. 'It must be very gratifying for you to see me reduced to supplicant like this. The tables turned, with a vengeance.'

'I'm not refusing out of spite,' she said, stung.

'Aren't you?' His eyes were scornful as he turned to look at her. 'Your body says one thing and your mind another. Your physical response appears to be something you can't control as easily as that independent mind of yours. Why can't you just follow your instincts and to hell with the thought processes for once?'

'I already did that,' Theo pointed out. 'I don't intend to repeat the experience.'

'Then there's not much more to say, is there?' James bent to pat the dog. 'Take good care of her, mutt.' The smile he gave her as he straightened made her heart lurch. 'It seems such a waste, somehow. You're such a warm, lovely creature, Theodora Grace, and yet you'd rather write love scenes than take part in them for real.'

She nodded silently, unable to trust her voice.

'Goodbye, then, Theodora.'

'Goodbye, James.'

There was a tense, silent pause, and for a moment Theo was sure James was about to plead with her one last time, then he shrugged and went to the door without a word, closing it behind him with care.

Theo picked up the puppy and held him close as she listened to the car driving away. For some time she stayed where she was, exactly as James had left her, feeling shaken and depressed and wishing she had never set eyes on him. After a time she put down the wriggling dog and tried to bury herself in a book, but it was impossible to concentrate. She would never have believed it possible to want a man so much physically, and certainly not in his absence. Furious with disgust, she went off to have a bath once Jason was settled in the kitchen, running the water as scalding hot as her skin could bear. She scrubbed herself from head to toe in an attempt to evict the frustration still gnawing at her, an occupation that served to render her even less amenable than before to James Hackett's persuasion.

In the weeks that followed it seemed ironic that Edwina's relationship with Miles Hay progressed by leaps and bounds, while Theo wrestled with the realisation that her life lacked something only James could provide. Late spring came to Bedington, and with it an increased restlessness that irked Theo to the point where she was sorely tempted to ring James and tell him she was ready to give in. Only the fear that he might have changed his mind kept her back. She occupied herself by typing furiously, and walking a lot with Jason, taunted by those 'darling buds of May' which seemed to mock her self-imposed isolation as she wandered through a coutryside so burgeoning with life it made the contrast with her own more painful. Her nights grew more and more restless. Long, wakeful hours were spent in convincing herself that her writing was fulfilment enough, that she needed nothing more.

'You look like hell!' said Edwina bluntly one weekend. 'You need a break.'

Theo shook her head. 'Must finish the book.'

'It looks as though it's finishing you!' The bright eyes were searching as Edwina fondled Jason. 'Darling— forgive me if I'm interfering, but as a mere aunt I feel I must. Letty doesn't dare. Nevertheless, we're all very worried.'

'Why? I'm leading an exemplary enough life, surely!'

'That's the worrying bit. Life shouldn't be so exemplary at your age, Theo. It's not good for you.'

'I need the peace and quiet to write,' said Theo stubbornly.

'And when you finish the book?'

'I don't know, Edwina. Maybe I'll have a little holiday.'

'Abroad?'

Theo laughed. 'Too expensive.'

Edwina hesitated. 'You're not, well, put out about Miles and me, by any chance?'

Theo stared at her blankly, then grinned. 'No, Auntie darling. You and Miles are free to make hay as much— oh, sorry, no pun intended!'

Edwina still looked concerned. 'Then tell me the reason for the pale and interesting look about you lately. The cottage isn't haunted, is it?'

'Not by a ghost,' said Theo rashly, then went bright red at Edwina's instant look of comprehension.

'Then you're pining for James,' she said promptly.

'No, I am not!'

Denials were useless. Edwina was quite relentless at ferreting out the truth, not satisfied until Theo admitted she missed the man a little. Upon which Edwina delivered a trenchant lecture on the brevity of life, and gave her niece a free, unsolicited opinion that she was lacking in grey matter not to see the man occasionally since *not* seeing him was so obviously causing distress.

'He doesn't want just to *see* me, Edwina,' Theo said pointedly.

'Well, no, love, I didn't think he did.'

'He wants me to live with him, let him rule my life, and I'm just not having any.' Theo's eyes flashed. 'He actually had the effrontery to suggest spending just the weekends together if that was the only way I'd consent.'

'Rather sensible,' approved Edwina. 'Work during the week, then play at weekends. More or less what I do, really. But you said no,' she added, resigned.

'Of course I said no!'

'Why?'

Theo glared at her aunt in exasperation. 'I'm not going to be someone's part-time playmate.'

'But you said you didn't want James to take over your entire life—surely this way would suit you down to the ground.'

'Edwina, just shut up, would you?'

'Oh, very well. Let's take Jason for a walk.'

But as they strolled through the pale, tender green of the May evening Edwina kept harping on the subject until Theo threatened physical violence if her aunt kept on.

'It's over,' she said flatly. 'I haven't heard from James for months now. He's finally seen the light.' At which thought she looked so stricken that Edwina hurried her back to the cottage and plied her with several glasses of wine over supper to cheer her up.

Long after Edwina left the next day for London and Miles, Theo kept hearing her stricture about enjoying life, and though conscious she should disapprove, agreed with Edwina's views far more than she let on. After her manuscript had been sent off, she finally decided, she would ask the Cowpers to put her up for a night or two at Willow Lodge, and do her best to engineer an accidental meeting with James. Much cheered by this decision, she got on with her typing at a great rate during the next few days. Her walks with Jason were suddenly highly enjoyable affairs, and on the stretch of open common ground where he could run free off the leash she ran with him, collapsing in a heap with him, laughing and breathless as he barked in excitement and licked her face to demonstrate how much he loved her.

One evening Theo and Jason were on their way back to the cottage with supper in mind, when the telephone

could be heard as they came through the garden gate.
Theo tore into the house but by the time she reached it
the telephone had stoppped ringing.

'Botheration!' said Theo, scowling, and went off to
free Jason of his choke chain. 'Probably Mother,' she
told him.

A little later the telephone rang again and Theo ran to
pick it up.

'Is that Miss Grace?' asked a voice, feminine and
rather musical, and quite unfamiliar.

'Yes,' said Theo, mystified.

'My name is Bronwen Hackett.'

Theo almost dropped the receiver.

'Are you there, Miss Grace?' said the voice,

'Yes—yes, Mrs Hackett,' said Theo breathlessly.

'I'm ringing to tell you that my son has met with an
accident.'

Theo went cold. 'James? Please—Mrs Hackett, what
happened? Is he——'

'He was on the site of the new office block and fell—
are you still there?'

Theo's teeth began to chatter. 'Yes,' she said with
difficulty. 'I'm still here. Is—is he all right?'

Mrs Hackett's voice sounded strained. 'He's home
from the hospital. They did all they could for him.'

'*What?* I mean, how is he?'

'He's asking for you, Miss Grace. Theodora, isn't it?'

'Yes.'

'Will you come? Please?'

'Yes—yes. Tell him I'm on my way.'

Her hand shaking like someone with palsy, Theo
scribbled down the address of the house near Roath Park
in Cardiff, promising to get there as quickly as she could,
and put down the telephone feeling utterly shattered.
For once she cursed her own refusal to learn to drive. At

that moment she would have sold her soul for the ability to jump in a car and head for the Severn Bridge as fast as the speed limits would allow. Instead she rang her father who, calm as always, said he would come at once to collect her and deposit her at the station in Cheltenham. His first response had been an offer to drive her to Cardiff, but Theo refused, despite her gratitude, and asked him to have Jason for her instead.

She threw a few things in an overnight bag and changed into the first dress to hand, but her brain refused to function normally in her frenzy of anxiety about James. Fortunately Letty Grace arrived with her husband and took charge of basic things like putting out a note for the milkman and collecting Jason's belongings together for his unexpected stay in Cheltenham.

'Is James bad?' asked Mrs Grace briefly.

'I don't know. They've sent him home from hospital and he's asking for me,' said her daughter, white-lipped, and her parents said no more on the journey, and stayed with her on the platform until the 7.59 to Cardiff put in an appearance.

'I'll ring,' said Theo tersely, as she said goodbye. 'And thank you—for everything.'

The train journey was a nightmare. The entire way Theo was racked with fear over the things Mrs Hacket had left unsaid. Suppose James was worse, that she failed to get there in time? At the thought the colour left Theo's face to such a degree the man opposite leapt up to open the window, convinced she was about to faint.

At Cardiff Central station, Theo ran swiftly to the taxi rank and gave Mrs Hackett's address, oblivious to her surroundings in the dusk as she was driven to her destination. When the taxi stopped in a tree-lined cul-de-sac of old, three-storeyed houses, Theo paid the driver and carried her overnight bag through a wrought-iron gate. She walked with suddenly reluctant feet along a path curving through a small front lawn. The night was warm, but Theo shivered as she reached the porch of the large, bay-windowed house. There was a bell push beside the open outer door, but before she could reach a hand to it an inner door, inlaid with stained-glass panels, swung open. The slim, grey-haired woman smiling at her in welcome was so like James there was no question of her identity.

'I'm Theodora Grace,' volunteered Theo, swallowing hard.

'How do you do, my dear? Come in, come in.' Bronwen Hackett took Theo's cold hand and drew her into a long, dim hall, where red Turkey carpet ran the length of the black and white mosaic floor. Theo saw nothing but the compassionate dark eyes of James's mother. Dark eyes, not blue, she thought dimly. They should be blue.

'You're trembling,' said Mrs Hackett, concerned. 'Come and sit down and have some hot tea. You could do with it, I'm sure, after that old train.'

Tea? Theo stared blankly, then shook her head. 'Nothing, thank you Mrs Hackett—I just want to see James. May I?'

'He's asleep at the moment, at long last.' Bronwen Hackett sighed, then shrugged. 'All right, my dear. Better to get it over with, I suppose.'

Theo's heart plummeted. As she followed Mrs Hackett up the stairs her knees were trembling so much she had to support herself with a hand on the satin-smooth mahogany of the banister rail. They reached a landing which seemed, to Theo's dazed eyes, lined with closed doors except for one which stood ajar at the far end. Mrs Hackett led her to it and silently motioned Theo to enter, then withdrew to go back downstairs, leaving her guest alone with her son.

The bedroom looked huge and shadowy, lit only by a small beside lamp. In the wide bed James lay on his back, still and silent as an effigy. His aquiline profile stood out in sharp relief against the dim glow, a white dressing on his forehead in stark contrast to the darkness of his skin. Theo bit hard on her lip to calm herself. Odd how she had expected him to be pale, when she knew well enough he was always tanned, summer and winter. The duvet covering him reached only to his chest, leaving his arms and shoulders bare, and he looked unexpectedly defenceless lying there so tidily, his breathing very quiet. Theo winced at the sight of a bruise beneath one eye, spreading darkly over his cheekbone, and she leaned closer, noting with a pang how weary he looked. She wondered if he had other injuries she couldn't see, whether there were internal ones his mother hadn't mentioned, then her heart skipped a beat as the black lashes lifted slowly and the familiar blue eyes stared uncomprehendingly into hers. At once the lids dropped and opened again, and the black brows drew together in amazement.

'Theodora?' whispered James in wonder.

'Yes——' Theo got no further, except for a little screech of shock as James shot bolt upright in bed and seized her by the shoulders in a grip of iron.

'You came,' he muttered indistinctly, and dragged her towards him, his mouth coming down on hers with a groan as he held her cruelly tight against his bare chest. For a split second Theo lay in his arms, stunned. Then, she pulled herself together and shoved him away to scramble off the bed, her eyes blazing with anger in her flushed face as she thrust her hair behind her ears with fingers that shook with fury.

'I thought you were *dying*!' she spat in rage. 'Is this

your idea of a joke, James Hackett?'

James propped himself on his hands, his eyes unrepentant. 'I *was* dying! Dying for the sight and sound and feel of you, Theodora.'

'Of all the rotten, despicable, low-down tricks to pull!' Her voice fairly vibrated with rage as she hugged her arms across her chest to stop shaking. She felt sick with fury, embarrassment, relief—so many emotions warred inside her she could have blacked James Hackett's good eye with the utmost relish.

'I would have stooped to any trick in the book to prove you cared for me.' James's eyes blazed into hers. 'My little mishap provided an opportunity too good to pass up. And it worked—you came running.'

'Oh—you—you——' Theo flung away to storm from the room and narrowly avoided colliding with Mrs Hackett in the doorway.

'And I was his accomplice,' said that lady calmly, steadying Theo as she stumbled. 'There, there, my dear, gently now. You've had a shock, I know. If it's any consolation, I hated deceiving you like that.'

It was difficult to rage at a much older woman whom she had only just met, and Theo fought down the anger threatening to get out of hand. 'I'm sure you had your reasons, Mrs Hackett,' she said stiffly, ignoring James, 'but now I think I'll take my leave. Your son has had his little joke, and I'll just ring for a taxi, if I may——'

'Certainly not, at this time of night,' said Mrs Hackett firmly, and put an arm round Theo's waist soothingly. She sent a spear-like glance at her watchful son. 'I was thoroughly opposed to the idea from the start. Frightening the poor girl like that—I told you she'd be mad with you, James.'

'Tell her why you gave in and helped, Bron,' said James urgently. 'Please listen, Theodora.'

Theo looked from the man in the bed, with his eyes dangerously bright in his haggard, bruised face, to the serene features of the woman beside her, and nodded silently.

Mrs Hackett sighed. 'One day, Miss Grace, you'll probably have children yourself. If you do, you'll find out that when they get hurt you'll do anything in the world you can to make it better. When they're babies you can kiss it better most times. When it's a grown man with a crack on his head and concussion that made him shout for someone called Theodora all night you stoop to half-truths and subterfuge to achieve the necessary result.'

As she listened to Bronwen Hackett's deep, musical voice explaining her devotion to her son Theo relaxed, the anger and tension inside her easing gradually. Reaction followed in their wake, and with it, to her intense mortification, tears. All at once everything was too much, and she put her hands to her face and wept, and with a muffled sound James heaved himself out of the bed, then stopped, swaying, his hand clapped to his head. With an exclamation his mother pushed him back down on the bed, and pulled the duvet over him.

'What a pair!' she said, shaking her head. 'You, my son, can just stay where you are and keep quiet for a bit, do you hear? Theodora, you come with me.'

'Bron!' howled James in protest, but his mother was unmoved as she plumped up his pillows and made him comfortable, then led Theo purposefully from the room.

'You wash your face,' she told Theo kindly. 'Bathroom at the head of the stairs. Then come straight down to the drawing-room—it's the one at the front—and have a cup of tea and a bite to eat, there's a good girl.'

Obediently Theo did as she was told, and alone in the bathroom had her cry out, blew her nose and washed her face. When she emerged she cast a black look along the landing towards James's room, then went downstairs. She turned the white porcelain knob on the drawing-room door and paused before entering, blinking. Unlike James's bedroom, with its thick, new carpet, and modern king-sized bed, or even the refurbished bathroom, the room she was staring at was straight out of another era. Chairs and sofas upholstered in black and silver Chinese brocade stood on a carpet the same shade of dull violet as the velvet curtains looped back from the great bay window with tasselled silver cords. A black lacquer cabinet stood against one wall, filled with pieces of jade and ruby glass, Meissen china figures and Chinese porcelain plates. The other walls were almost obscured by pictures in heavy gilt frames. Oil paintings of Highland cattle and dead game hung next to water colours of Venetian scenes and pen-and-ink drawings of Welsh castles. Above the marble mantelpiece two gilt-framed sepia photographs dominated the room, an autocratic gentleman with a beak of a nose and heavy moustache and a lady with a heroic bust and a calm face surmounted by the fringe of curls made fashionable by Queen Alexandra.

'My grandparents,' said Bronwen Hackett, wheeling in an incongruously modern tea trolley. 'Now sit down and take some of these sandwiches. A nice bit of salmon—fresh, mind—and cucumber and cress. What do you think of the room?'

Theo sat down in one of the brocade chairs, mentally taking note of her surroundings for future use. 'It's like being in a time capsule, or on the set of one of those period television serials.'

Mrs Hackett nodded as she poured out. 'Never been changed since it was redecorated at the time of the coronation. King George and Queen Mary's, that is.

Royal purple was the rage, not to mention all this chinoiserie. My grandmother was never one for half measures.'

After her excess of emotion Theo found she was quite hungry, and enjoyed her sandwich more than she'd anticipated. 'But how on earth do you manage to keep it like this?' she asked.

'With great difficulty.' Mrs Hackett passed her a cup of tea, then looked about her with gloom.

'But you love it!'

'I do not!' was the surprising answer. 'The room's a museum piece, that's all. I was never allowed inside it as a child. Then when I was left the house a year or so ago——'

'So you haven't lived here all your life?'

'Dear me, no. I was shown the door thirty-six years ago and told never to darken it again.' Bronwen Hackett smiled. 'But don't let a garrulous old woman bore you with tales of the past. It's a habit one gets into without realising it, I'm afraid.'

Theo was rapidly regaining herself under the influence of the food and the calm conversation she suspected was intended for that very purpose. She was no longer frantic with worry about James, and the anguish of the day, and even her recent shock, had receded, making it easier for her to sympathise with Bronwen Hackett's motives for frightening her so badly. She smiled at her hostess with more warmth.

'In actual fact I'm very partial to tales of the past, Mrs Hackett. I don't suppose James has mentioned it, but I've written a period novel myself.'

'Oh yes, he certainly mentioned it. In fact he gave me your book to read a few weeks ago, and I enjoyed it very much. You're a very talented young woman.' The dark eyes gleamed suddenly. 'The hero was a bit familiar, mind!'

'Loosely based on your son,' admitted Theo ruefully. 'With a few subtle additions, I think.'

They exchanged smiles in accord, then Theo asked hesitantly. 'Why did your father show you the door? Or is it too painful? And am I being much too inquisitive?' she added hurriedly.

'No, of course not. I brought it up.' Mrs Hackett's eyes took on a distant, remembering look. 'I met a man, you see. Ralph Hackett, James's father, with his blue, philandering eyes. Now my father, and his before him, were coal merchants, successful and respectable to the core. But Ralph was a small-time builder—very small—and neither of those things, and not even Welsh. Instead of a house like this, my married life, such as it was, was spent in a small semi in the Midlands, one of rows of others just like it stretching in every direction. James made his escape when he went to college, and never came back, really. Not long after, I sold the house and bought a flat down here, back to my roots, and even saw my mother in secret. My father never relented, I'm sad to say, so it was a big surprise to find he'd left the house to me, after all. James wanted me to sell it, but I decided to move back here instead.'

Theo took a Welshcake from the dish her hostess offered and bit into it. 'Mm—delicious!' She looked at Mrs Hackett curiously. 'But aren't you lonely here? It's a big house to live in alone.'

'I'm a very self-sufficient woman,' declared Mrs Hackett. 'But then, so are you, James tells me.'

'I like to think so.' Theo coloured a little as she met Bronwen Hackett's eyes very squarely. 'I do apologise for making such a scene upstairs—not for getting angry, because I think I was justified—but for the tears and so on. Not my usual style.'

'No. I don't imagine they are.'

'But it was such a shock when James sat bolt upright and grabbed me.'

'Like a corpse coming to life!'

Theo shuddered at the thought. 'What exactly *did* happen to James, Mrs Hackett?' she asked.

Mrs Hackett chuckled. 'Something so stupid he gets furious every time he thinks of it. He slipped in some mud on the site, his helmet flew off and he hit his head on an upright of the scaffolding. Result, a gash on the head and a black eye, and instead of getting treatment right away the idiot got in his car and drove down the M4 to me, concussion and all. God knows how he didn't kill himself. I called in my doctor who immediately took him to the casualty department at Heath Hospital where James was duly X-rayed and stitched up and finally returned to me. He kept me awake all night calling for you in his sleep.'

'So that part was true?'

'I never actually lied to you, Theodora.'

'But you managed to frighten me to death, just the same!'

'I'm sorry for that, my dear, but James was hot and restless and I acted on impulse, hoping to provide him with the cure he seemed to need.' The dark eyes scrutinised Theo curiously. 'I was very curious to meet you. You're a very good-looking girl, but what exactly do you possess that makes you so different from all the rest, I wonder?'

Theo's eyes narrowed warily. 'What do you mean?'

'James's sole problem with the opposite sex up to now has been a superfluity of numbers. But you, he tells me, won't have him.'

'You've got it. That's what makes me different from the others.'

'Why won't you have him?'

'I know him too well. I worked for him for eighteen months, you know.'

'Yes, James told me some extraordinary story about making yourself look a fright to get the job.'

Theo flushed. 'Silly of me, wasn't it? I'd heard he wanted someone unlikely to prove vulnerable to the famous Hackett charm so I disguised myself a little. It worked like a charm, and, God knows, I worked, too, like a slave.' She met Bronwen Hackett's eyes with candour. 'Your son, Mrs Hackett, can be a pig at times to work for. If you're a female, that is. He deals very well with his own sex.'

'Presumably because they don't fall in love with him!' Mrs Hackett leaned forward to take Theo's plate. 'So you left him eventually because he treated you so badly.'

'No, not exactly. Rather the reverse. By sheer accident he found out what I look like normally and began to take too much interest in me.'

'Oh, I see! He made a pass and you walked out.'

'In a way. But then, you see, I had always intended to leave once my book was accepted, providing such a miracle should occur. When it did I wanted to concentrate solely on my writing. I'd already proved how difficult it was to write *and* work for James at the same time.'

Mrs Hackett sighed. 'Couldn't you write your novels and just be married to James?'

Theo laughed shortly. 'Oh, he doesn't want to *marry* me, Mrs Hackett. He just wants to sleep with me.'

'He actually said that!'

'More or less. The idea is that I live with him until such time as the arrangement ceases to please him, whereupon he will provide me with a place of my own and a lump sum in compensation, as I remember it.'

Bronwen Hackett groaned. 'And this was *before* he had the crack on his head! Stupid boy.'

Theo shrugged. 'And what should I do now, do you think?'

'What do you want to do, my dear?'

Crawl into bed with James and sleep the clock round, thought Theo secretly. Aloud she said, 'I'm not sure.'

Mrs Hackett rose to her feet. 'Think about it in the morning. In the meantime I've put your bag in the room next to James. I'm along the landing in my old room next to the bathroom. It's very late and one way and another I should think you're quite worn out, so run upstairs and say goodnight to my son, who is no doubt going off his head up there, wondering what we're talking about. I'll bring you both a hot drink in a little while, then you can get a good night's sleep.'

Theo thanked her hostess, asking permission to ring her parents briefly, then went up the stairs afterwards to the cool, pot-pourri-scented upper landing, and James's bedroom. He was lying on his back, an arm thrown across his eyes. Theo closed the door quietly and James spoke wearily, not looking in her direction.

'She left then, Bron?'

'No. I didn't.'

James flung the arm away and twisted in the bed to look at her with incredulous eyes. 'You stayed?'

'It looks very much like it.' She sat on the edge of the bed. 'It seemed the sensible thing to do once I'd calmed down a bit. How's your head?'

He lifted one shoulder indifferently. 'Aches a bit. I'll probably be all right tomorrow.'

'I hear you called for me in the night,' she said quietly.

His jaw clenched. 'Bron shouldn't have told you.'

'It's the reason she gave for asking me to come. She thought seeing me would calm you down.'

'Calm me down!' His lips took on a bitter twist. 'I can't say the sight of you ever does that, exactly!' His eyes met hers and they stared at each other in silence. 'So why did you come, Theodora?' he asked at last.

'I thought I was rushing to your death bed.'

'A bit disappointing to find my bed occupied by someone very much alive, then.'

'No, not really.'

James's eyes narrowed. 'What do you mean?'

Theo examined her fingernails with care. 'More or less what you think I mean, I suppose.'

His hand shot out to grasp hers, his fingers tightening cruelly. 'Theodora, look at me.'

She obeyed, her eyes unveiled, and with a sharp intake of breath James drew her slowly towards him. 'I can't believe this is really happening,' he muttered hoarsely, his eyes feverishly bright. 'You're not a hallucination are you, darling? Concussion does strange things I gather.'

'Shall I pinch you?' Theo offered helpfully, and leaned to take his ear lobe between her finger and thumb.

The featherlight touch was too much for James. He caught both her hands and she slid across the duvet into his arms, offering up her face for the kisses he pressed all over it hungrily, until she put up a hand and brought his head down so that his mouth was on hers where she wanted it. He groaned against her parted lips and kissed her with a longing so intense, Theo took fright in case the excess of emotion should prove bad for him.

'Softly, James,' she said raggedly, smoothing back his hair with a gentle hand. 'Let's not have you back in hospital.'

'If I go, you go too,' he said huskily, but subsided obediently to her surprise, drawing her close so that they

lay cheek to cheek on the pillow, their arms about each
other in a fragile sort of peace. Then the door opened.

'I did knock,' announced Mrs Hackett. 'But I don't
think you heard me.' She put a tray down on the bedside
table as Theo, her colour high, tried to free herself.
James kept her firmly where she was.

'Quite respectable and above board, Bron,' he assured
his mother. 'Theodora's on top of the covers and I'm out
of harm's way underneath.'

'That old concussion must be worse than I thought,'
said Mrs Hackett, shaking her head. 'A changed man,
that's what you are.'

Theo giggled, and the other woman nodded apprais-
ingly. 'That's better. Thought I'd never get a laugh out
of you. There's hot milk in this flask, mind. So both of
you have some and then get some sleep.'

'Hot milk!' James scowled in disgust.

'I put a little something in it to ginger it up. Do both of
you good.' Mrs Hackett bent to kiss them both. 'Right,
then. Goodnight to the pair of you. I'm off to bed.'

Theo sat up and smiled at her. 'Goodnight, Mrs
Hackett—and I'm glad you rang me.'

'Good.' Bronwen nodded approvingly and went to the
door. 'I was brought up to tell the truth, but God will
forgive me for lying by inference, don't you think, since
my motive was help for that bone-headed son of mine.
Goodnight.'

'Why bone-headed?' demanded James, aggrieved,
after his mother had gone.

Theo slid off the bed, not looking at him. 'I told her
about your proposition.'

'And Bron's Nonconformist upbringing rose up in
revolt because I asked you to live in sin, I suppose.'

'I think it was the pensioning-off bit when you tired of
me that rather made her blink.'

'When I said that I had no idea you were likely to become a fixture in my life, did I?'

Theo stared at him suspiciously. 'A fixture? A bit hard to swallow when I haven't heard a word from you for ages. I thought you'd given me up as a lost cause.'

'I had a bloody good try,' he said glumly, and hoisted himself higher against the pillows. 'Then after long and serious thought I came to the conclusion it wasn't such a good idea for you to move in with me after all.'

Theo became very busy with filling two mugs with the hot milk, rather pleased to find her hand so steady. 'I see,' she said, and turned to hand James one before tasting her own drink cautiously.

'I don't think you do.' He wrinkled his nose in distaste. 'Hot milk, for God's sake—can't I have something stronger?'

'It's less innocuous than it looks.' Theo rolled some of the liquid on her tongue. 'There's a fair lacing of rum in it, at a guess.'

Whatever was in the potion helped Theo cope with the sharp pain experienced over James's change of heart—or mind. 'So you don't want me for room-mate any more then?' she asked flippantly.

'Not precisely what I said.' James drained his drink and handed her the mug. 'Come over here,' he ordered, with a flash of the autocratic James she knew so well. Eyeing him warily Theo sat on the edge of the bed, near enough for him to capture her hand. James was quiet for a while, looking at the slim, capable hand he held, stroking her fingers gently. It was very quiet in the house. Theo heard the clock in the downstairs hall strike midnight as she sat patiently, waiting for James to speak.

'Theodora,' he said quietly at last. 'Since I saw you last I've had a lot of time to think.'

'About the company?'

'There's always that. I'd be lying if I denied it. You know me too well, anyway. But you're the one who's occupied my mind far more than Hackett Construction. After all, I do have some measure of control over the company. But where you're concerned I'm helpless.' He met her eyes squarely. 'I've been worried. For the first time in my life I can't sleep at night, worrying over whether you're safe in that cottage on your own, miles from anywhere, whether you're eating properly, taking good care of yourself—and most of all, whether some man is helping you with research for the love scenes in your new book.'

Theo glared at him, and tried to pull her hand away, but his fingers tightened. Even in the dim light the blaze in his eyes affected her strongly and she shook her head dumbly.

'What exactly are you denying, Theodora?' he asked quickly.

'No men, James. None at all, except Miles Hay occasionally, and from the moment he clapped eyes on Edwina she's the one he comes to see.'

James frowned. 'The editor and your aunt? Do you mind?'

'Not in the least. I've liked Miles from the start, but not——' Theo stopped abruptly.

'Not what?'

'Well, in just a friendly way. Professional even. Nothing more.'

'I wish I'd known that the day I saw you with him in London. I could have knocked his teeth down his throat!' His vehemence was both gratifying and unsetting, and Theo changed the subject.

'Are you going to build a house for Chloë Masson?'

'Yes. Not your sort of thing, at a guess—jacuzzis and saunas and so on.'

'So her husband's wealthy.'

'And elderly.'

Theo nodded. 'As you said, not my type of set-up all round.' She smiled cheerfully. 'You must be tired, James. I'd better go to bed and let you sleep.'

'Not until you've listened to what I have to say,' he said flatly.

'Very well. I'm listening.'

James smiled at her quizzically. 'Unlike Chloë, I gather you don't fancy being an old man's darling. You know what the alternative's said to be?'

'A young man's slave. I've had some of that,' she said tartly. 'Working for you is the nearest thing to slavery I ever intend to know.'

'I'm not asking you to work for me, Theodora.' Suddenly James was in deadly earnest. A pulse throbbed at the corner of his mouth. 'I want you to marry me.'

Theo blinked, hardly able to believe her own ears. '*Marry* you? But—you don't believe in marriage!'

'I've come to the conclusion that for you and me it's the only solution,' he said with finality.

'Solution! I'm not some engineering problem, James.' Her eyes dropped, and she turned away from the probing blue eyes. 'I'm not at all sure that marriage is what I want, anyway.'

'Neither am I. But if it's the only way I can have you, I'm willing to take the chance.' His hand tightened on hers and he began to pull her towards him, but she resisted, shaking her head vigorously.

'No, James. You've already proved quite conclusively how vulnerable I am to physical persuasion—yours, anyway. But there's more to marriage than bed.'

'I'm aware of that.' He smiled crookedly. 'But even a slave-driving egotist like me needs companionship, rapport, tolerance, the ability to laugh with someone.

None of the women in my life to date has ever done more than share my bed, spend my money and ultimately bore me stiff. You're different. Even discounting your looks, I like your intelligence, your common sense—even your independence. In a nutshell, life isn't the same without you.'

Theo stared blindly at the fingers stroking hers. Was marriage what she wanted after all?

'You're very quiet,' said James. 'Is the idea so astounding?'

'Yes.' Theo raised doubting eyes to his. 'And I'm not convinced it would work. You know how much I want to go on writing.'

'Of course I do. Can't you write and be married to me?'

'I don't know. I just don't know. I've only just started, really. I'm not likely to win critical acclaim for my efforts, but it seems I can easily earn my daily bread by doing something I enjoy to the full. But it's hard work, James. I get tired after writing all day. I don't think you'd put up with a wife whose only aim was a sandwich, bath and bed when you came home in the evenings.'

'I disagree,' said James promptly. 'As long as you wanted to share them with me I'd be only too happy.'

Theo's lips twitched. 'All three?'

'I'm not sold on the sandwich bit—I'd rather rustle up bacon and eggs myself. I'm a dab hand with a frying pan, you know!'

'No, I didn't.' She sighed deeply. 'But you'd need a lot of patience, James. And I know only too well it's not a virtue you possess.'

'Untrue. I'm exercising a great deal of patience right this minute.' His smile made her heart turn over. 'Surely you can tell that I'm fighting myself tooth and nail not to drag you in here beside me and make love to you until the only word you can think of is yes!'

'So why don't you?' asked Theo baldly.

James swallowed hard, his eyes glittering. 'That's not fair! I want all of you, not just your body, my darling. I want you to say yes because your brain wants to, not the kind of consent that's wrung out of you in the heat of the moment.'

Theo leaned forward impulsively and kissed him briefly. 'Very well, James. I'll sleep on it and give you my answer in the morning.'

He stared at her incredulously. 'You mean you're actually going to leave me in suspense all night?'

'Yes.'

'If you really wanted to marry me you'd have no hesitation,' he said bitterly. 'Women always know what they want.'

'As you've said before, one of the attractions I have for you is my dissimilarity to the other women you seem to attract.' Theo turned in the doorway, smiling at him cheerfully. 'See you in the morning.'

'I might be dead by then!'

'In which case the problem will be solved once and for all, won't it?'

CHAPTER TEN

THEO woke with a start during the night. She sat up, heart pounding, wondering what had disturbed her. She fumbled for the switch on the bedside lamp and slid out of Bronwen Hackett's spare bed, snatching up her dressing-gown as she made for the door.

Just outside on the landing she almost collided with James, who stood swaying, his face ghastly as Theo put out instinctive hands towards him as he began to fall. He was too big for her to stop him entirely, but somehow she managed to break his fall so that she landed with a thump in a sitting position with James sprawled over her, his head on her lap as his weight jammed her up against the wall. Bronwen Hackett came hurtling from her room and gave a gasp of horror as she fell to her knees beside her unconscious son. She gave a sharp look at Theo, who was struggling to get her breath back.

'Are you all right, love?'

Theo nodded breathlessly. 'A bit winded. I dashed out just in time to stop him crashing to the floor.' She winced and eased her position slightly as one of her legs began to go numb under James's weight.

'He must have gone to the bathroom. Stupid, isn't it, only one bathroom and seven bedrooms! I told him to ring the little bell I left with him, stubborn idiot.' Mrs Hackett smoothed the hair tenderly from her son's face. 'Thank God you were quick enough, Theodora. He might have needed a few more stitches otherwise.'

James stirred and groaned, clenching his teeth, and

175

Theo bent over him. 'What is it, darling?' she asked anxiously.

His eyes opened and looked up into hers. 'What happened?'

'You tell us!' said his mother tartly. 'I assume you went to the bathroom. Why didn't you call me?'

'No time,' he muttered. 'Felt sick.' He shuddered. 'I *was* sick, then afterward I felt dizzy. I keep telling you this house needs more bathrooms, Bron. Bloody barbaric having to walk miles.'

'I know, I know.' Mrs Hackett exchanged a worried glance with Theo. 'The thing is, how do we get you back to bed? You must be squashing Theodora.'

'I'm fine,' said Theo instantly.

'Nevertheless you can't stay like that all night.' Mrs Hackett sighed. 'Terrible invalid you are, James.'

'I'll get up now if you give me a hand,' James informed her firmly.

With grim determination he managed to get to his feet slowly, helped by the two protesting women, and, staggering slightly, finally gained the haven of his own bed, by which time there was a suspicious brightness to his eyes and a white line around his mouth.

'Now, for pity's sake stay put and go to sleep,' scolded his mother, her tartness a cover for her deep anxiety.

'I want Theodora to stay,' muttered James.

Theo shook her head. 'You need rest, not company. I'll see you in the morning.'

'Did I cause much damage when I crash-landed on top of you?'

'No, I'm still in one piece.' Theo smiled at him soothingly. 'Now sleep!'

'Come and see me first thing,' he commanded.

'Yes, Mr Hackett, sir!'

*   *   *

Bronwen Hackett let out a sigh of relief as she and Theo left the room. 'I need a cup of tea badly. How about you?'

Theo agreed fervently, and followed her hostess downstairs to a bright, modernised kitchen, where she sat limply at the table while Mrs Hackett made tea.

'That was a nasty shock,' commented Bronwen Hackett. 'I thought I heard something, but by the time I was out of bed you were both in a heap on the floor.'

'Some sixth sense prodded me awake, and I just ran.'

'Pity you didn't sleep with him!'

Theo coloured. 'My first thought when I found him,' she admitted. 'I could have been there when he needed me.'

'So why weren't you?' was the surprising response.

'I never have shared a bed with James yet, Mrs Hackett. It seemed bad manners to make a start under your roof, particularly after the talk I had with James after you went to bed.'

'Talk! Is that all you two can do? Things were different when I was a girl—which, of course, is why my father gave me my marching orders. I was expecting James before I got round to marrying his father.'

'Ah! I see.' Theo smiled sympathetically.

'Exactly. Father had strong views on keeping the conception of children to the confines of the legal marriage bed.' Bronwen Hackett gave a sudden mischievous smile. 'James was conceived on a bed of ferns and bluebells. Something very erotic about stars shining through branches of trees in a wood as you make love.'

Theo giggled helplessly. 'How utterly romantic!'

'There you are, then, make a note if it and use it in a book.' Mrs Hackett's face sobered and she sighed. 'The pity of it is, Theodora—are you always called that, by the way?'

'No. Just Theo.'

'Good. As I was saying, the sad part is that bluebells die and ferns turn to bracken, and my lover proved to be a weakling who squandered the money my father's conscience forced him to give me as a wedding present. Ralph started to knock me about—I hit him back, mind! Then James grew so big his father didn't dare hit him, or me, any more. Inevitably Ralph went bankrupt and rounded things off by leaving me for a woman who kept a public house, where he drank himself into an early grave.' Bronwen Hackett shrugged, her dark eyes ironic. 'It all left a lasting impression on my son regarding the sanctity—or lack of it—of marriage.'

Theo looked thoughtful. 'Yet he asked me to marry him tonight.'

'Good gracious! And what did you say to such a change of heart?'

'I said I'd sleep on it.'

'Sensible, but a trifle dampening for poor James!'

Theo smiled ruefully. 'I needed time to adjust. I made a sort of vow in the train. To God, I suppose. "Let James be all right and I'll be his lover for as long as he wants me" was the general theme. Highly unsuitable as a vow, no doubt. So it came as rather a shock to find James not only alive and more or less kicking, but talking about marriage into the bargain.'

'And?'

Theo sighed. 'I can't visualise the wife of James Hackett being able to write as easily as Theodora Grace, somehow.'

'Other women manage similar arrangements, with a few children thrown in,' said Mrs Hackett. 'The question is, my dear, do you love my son?'

'Oh, yes. If I'd had any doubts on the point they vanished the moment you told me he'd had an accident.'

Mrs Hackett smiled wisely, and patted Theo's hand. 'That's all that matters, really. Now you get off to bed and have a good sleep. Things will look different in the morning.'

The clock was striking three as Theo climbed the stairs wearily. She went quietly along the landing, and without turning on a light, took off her dressing-gown and slid into bed.

When she woke up the room was filled with a lambent, underwater light, as sunlight filtered through green blinds covering the windows. She turned her head on the pillow and smiled sleepily into the thunderstruck blue eyes regarding her from only a few inches away.

'I died and went to heaven?' enquired James.

Theo stretched luxuriously and rubbed her eyes, pushing the hair away from her face. 'No. I decided to make sure you didn't fall downstairs in the night. How's your head?'

'Not bad at all.' He moved closer. 'Tell me, Theodora. Have I missed anything? I remember you and Bron steering me back to bed, then nothing until a few minutes ago when I turned over to find you beside me.'

'That's all there is.' Theo yawned widely. 'You frightened the life out of me last night, so I came in here to make sure you didn't go walkabout again. It's a big bed. I didn't think I'd disturb you.'

'Pity the bed *is* so big,' he said huskily.

'Why? Would you like me to come closer?' she asked, quite plainly astonishing him as she slid across the intervening space and into his arms. For a second or two James remained rigid with shock, his heart hammering against her cheek. Then, with a muffled sound, he pressed her head into the hollow of his shoulder and held her tight.

'I'll never understand you, Theodora,' he muttered

into her hair. 'You have a positive talent for the unexpected.'

She freed her head to look up at him mischievously. 'I wanted to see what it was like—waking up with a man.'

'You've never slept with a man before?' The familiar pulse was throbbing at the corner of his mouth.

Theo put her lips against it. 'No. You need a shave.'

'That's not all I need,' he answered unsteadily.

She frowned at him. 'I thought you were dying yesterday. I nearly went out of my mind.'

James shook her slightly. 'Is that the truth?'

'Yes.'

He took in a deep, uneven breath. 'Even if I had been, one touch from you like this would have brought me back to life.'

She shuddered. 'Let's not ever put it to the test.'

'Useful, really,' he said lightly. 'We shan't need an alarm clock for a wedding present. The slightest touch from you in the morning and I'll be ready to start the day right.'

'How?'

'By making love to you so that you'll be fired with inspiration for your tales of passion.' James was teasing, but nevertheless, something in his voice sent prickles along Theo's spine.

'You don't have to marry me to do that,' she said huskily.

'I'm afraid I want exclusive rights or none at all.' James stared down at her, a look in his eyes she knew of old.

'Can't we just be lovers, James?' she asked, sighing. 'I'm not sure I can manage to be a wife and carry on writing. And I want so desperately to write.'

'And I so desperately want you to marry me.' His face went dark, and he flung over on to his back. 'Hell,

Theodora, every woman wants to get married, however much they make noises about equality and so on. Why the blazes must you be the only one to say no?'

'You told me you'd never asked anyone else.'

'I haven't. If I had they'd have said yes, I assure you!'

'Conceited oaf!'

They glared at each other, then with a curse James yanked her into his arms and began kissing her with fevered desperation. Theo struggled to pull away, tried not to respond, and failed miserably on both counts. After a time she managed to free her mouth.

'You said you wouldn't resort to—to this,' she panted.

'I've changed my mind,' he muttered hotly, and his lips silenced her again, his hand sliding beneath the satin of her pyjama jacket, his fingers flicking open the buttons. His mouth left hers to swoop downwards over her throat to close on a nipple that responded instantly to the suck of his lips and the delicate grazing of his teeth, and Theo writhed beneath the caress.

'Please——' she gasped. 'Don't——'

'Be quiet,' he grated, and rolled over on top of her, his body tense with demand above hers. 'Say you'll marry me,' he insisted against her open, gasping mouth.

'No——'

Ungentle hands relieved her of the pyjamas and James slid between her trembling knees and waited, poised. Theo shook her head from side to side blindly, then reared up against him as his fingers discovered exactly how much she wanted him. At last, when she thought she might die if he didn't take her, James spoke in her ear.

'Say it!'

'Yes, yes,' she said hoarsely, then to her outrage he rolled over to his side of the bed and lay with eyes closed, breathing hard. Instead of flying at him with her nails, as she wanted, Theo pulled on her pyjamas instead, then she noticed his tallow-pale face and tensed.

'What's wrong, James?'

He breathed in deeply several times before replying. 'I feel sick,' he said finally, through clenched teeth, and drops of perspiration rolled down his forehead to soak the dressing on his wound.

'Oh, God—shall I——?'

'Don't do anything,' he said tersely. 'I feel better now.'

Theo doubted the truth of this, and wrapped herself in her dressing-gown. 'I'll get you a glass of water,' she said, and flew along the landing to the bathroom to fill a glass, then raced back.

James sat up gingerly and drank a little of the water, then looked at her remorsefully. 'I'm sorry, Theodora.'

She sat on the edge of the bed, relaxing a little as James's colour improved. 'I thought you were being bloody-minded.'

'I don't have that much self-control, I promise you. If the dreaded nausea hadn't overtaken me at that precise moment, Miss Grace, by now you'd have been well and truly loved.'

Theo's face went poppy-red, and James grinned unrepentantly. 'I'm not known for my reticence in speaking my mind, as you well know! But there is something I want to say, if you'll listen.'

'I'm listening.'

James leaned forward to take her hand and looked deep into her eyes. 'It's difficult. Probably because I've never said it to a woman before. Just—I love you.'

Theo swallowed hard. 'Then why didn't you say so before? It's powerful persuasion when a man's proposing marriage, James Hackett.'

'Do you love me, Theodora?'

Her eyes dropped before the intensity of his, and she nodded dumbly.

He let out a deep breath and held her close. 'God only knows why. I know I'm not easy to love.'

Theo nodded vigorously in agreement. 'That's for sure. Sexy you may be, lovable you're not.'

They were laughing together when Mrs Hackett came in with a tea tray. 'Well, that's better,' she said. 'How are things this morning?'

Her son leaned back against the pillows Theo had been stacking behind him, and sighed with pleasure. 'Things couldn't be better, Bron, since you ask. Theodora has promised to be my wife.'

His mother beamed at them both. 'Persuaded you after all, did he, Theo?'

Theo exchanged glances with a smug James. 'I suppose you could put it like that!'

'And how do you feel this morning, son?'

'On top of the world, surprisingly. I felt a bit sick just now, but I think if I manage to avoid similar excitement in future I should be fit to marry Theodora in a week or so.'

'A week or so!' hooted Theo. 'You'll be lucky. I'm an only child, remember, and my mother's been planning my wedding since I left school. She'll insist on a church wedding with all the trimmings, James Hackett, so if you want to back out, now's the time to say so.'

'Nonsense,' said Mrs Hackett. 'I agree with your mother strongly. I'd like to meet her—and your father, of course.'

'Oh, God,' groaned James. 'I'd thought of something quick and simple then off to the sun for a honeymoon.'

'First the penny then the bun,' said Mrs Hackett firmly.

Later that day, when Bronwen Hackett was out

shopping, James insisted on dressing and going downstairs to sit with Theo in the small, comfortable little sitting-room, with the french windows open to the sunshine in the walled garden at the back of the house.

'A bit cosier here than the drawing-room,' remarked Theo idly, as she lay curled against James, her head on his shoulder.

'Bron took you in there last night?' James asked in surprise. 'You must have thought you were in Cardiff Museum.'

'I think she was giving me time to get over my shock, and that room is certainly a conversation piece. My mother would be most impressed.'

'Ghastly, in my opinion. It's only ever been used for funerals.'

Theo chuckled, and wriggled closer. 'Where shall *we* live?'

'Anywhere you want. I'll build you a house if you like.'

'Would you?' breathed Theo, impressed.

'Certainly, madam. A study with a view of the garden, so you can write your masterpieces, a nice kitchen where you can cook, and a *very* nice big bedroom where you can make love to me.' His voice roughened on the last and Theo quivered.

'Don't let's even think about that, you might feel sick again.'

'God, you're a romantic little soul, darling!'

'Practical, that's me. Anyway, your mother might come in and I don't care for being caught in the act, if you cast your mind back to another occasion.'

James's face assumed a pious expression somewhat at odds with his black eye. 'I had no intention of making love to you. In fact, I refuse to let you have your wicked way with me again at all until you're entitled to the privilege in the eyes of church and law.'

Theo tried to hide her dismay as she stared at him. 'But it may be a couple of months at least before we can get married, you know.'

'Two months!' James wavered, then his face took on a mulish look Theo recognised with misgiving. 'No matter. I've made up my mind. The next time I make love to you will be when you're Mrs James Hackett.'

'"Within the legal confines of the marriage bed",' quoted Theo heavily.

'Well, yes,' he agreed, eyeing her in surprise.

Theo was very quiet for some time, digesting the fact that now she had given in and consented to marry James, two months was likely to be a very long time. Her own plan of just living together would have meant sharing a bed from the start, but now James had committed himself to marriage he appeared to have developed an obstinately puritanical streak. Taking after his grandfather, thought Theo morosely, and jumped up restlessly to go over to the open doors, looking out at the pink, frothy blossom on the flowering cherry in the garden.

'Will you be well enough to come to the cottage this weekend, James?' she asked casually.

'Yes, of course. How about your aunt?'

'There's plenty of room. Bring your mother, too, then she can meet up with my parents, as she asked.'

James laughed, and got to his feet to stand behind her, sliding an arm round her waist to pull her back against him. He leaned his chin on her hair. 'So we'll be heavily chaperoned.'

'If we want time to ourselves we can always go for walks. The woods near the cottage are lovely this time of the year,' said Theo pensively.

'Sounds good. I haven't been walking in the woods for

years.' He breathed in the scent of her hair with appreciation, then sighed deeply. 'Just think of all the things we can do together for the first time, sweetheart. Like reading together in front of the fire——'

'Washing up——'

'Digging the garden——'

'Shovelling snow——'

'Entertaining friends to dinner——'

Involuntarily they turned to each other and Theo held up her mouth. James bent his head and held her close, his kiss growing harder and fiercer as she yielded to him in a new, compliant way that plainly went to his head. At last he held her away from him, breathing hard, and looked possessively at her flushed face.

'Theodora Grace, I love you so much it's going to be bloody difficult to keep to my vow of abstinence.'

'Makes the heart grow fonder,' she murmured, and kissed the warm skin of his throat, delighting in his sharp intake of breath.

'I couldn't keep my hands off you when you were cold and distant,' he said raggedly. 'How am I going to wait for months when you behave like this, you witch?'

Her smile was innocent. 'A big strong man like you, James Hackett? Where's that iron resolution of yours?'

'Conspicuous by its absence when you smile at me like that!'

She leaned against him deliberately. 'Perhaps I'd better go back tomorrow, out of harm's way. Then you'll be quite safe—and when we're at the cottage, since we'll be surrounded by people the whole time!'

'Not on your life!' He laughed and hugged her hard, then sighed. 'I'll just have to pray for fine weather, so I can nurture a passion for the great outdoors, instead of battling with a passion for you, my lovely.'

A tiny smile tugged at the corners of Theo's mouth.

'The fresh air will do us good, darling. Besides, at this time of the year the woods are carpeted with ferns and bluebells, and in the evenings one can watch the stars come out one by one through the branches of the trees . . .' She broke off, flushing bright red as she caught sight of Mrs Hackett standing just outside, her face wreathed in smiles as she listened.

'Feeling better then, son?' Mrs Hackett asked James, and patted Theo's cheek as she came into the room.

'Wonderful,' said James with emphasis, and drew Theo close as he grinned at his mother. 'I had a fight to make her say yes, but I won in the end. You approve of my choice of wife, I trust?' he added.

'Would it make a blind bit of difference if I didn't?' she demanded.

Theo laughed delightedly. 'How well you know your son!'

'As well as any mother knows her son, I suppose.' Bronwen Hackett winked at Theo outrageously, then smiled at James reassuringly. 'But since you ask, son, from what I heard her saying just now I'd say your future wife's a girl after my own heart!'

Take 4 best-selling love stories FREE
Plus get a FREE surprise gift!

ATTRACTIVE, SPACE SAVING BOOK RACK

Display your most prized novels on this handsome and sturdy book rack. The hand-rubbed walnut finish will blend into your library decor with quiet elegance, providing a practical organizer for your favorite hard-or soft-covered books.

Only $9.95

Approximately 16" x 8" when assembled

Assembles in seconds!

To order, rush your name, address and zip code, along with a check or money order for $10.70* ($9.95 plus 75¢ postage and handling) payable to *Harlequin Reader Service*:

Harlequin Reader Service
Book Rack Offer
901 Fuhrmann Blvd.
P.O. Box 1396
Buffalo, NY 14269-1396

Offer not available in Canada.

BKR-1A

*New York and Iowa residents add appropriate sales tax.

MAIL-IN-OFFER
OFFER CERTIFICATE ✂

I have enclosed the required number of proofs of purchase from any specially marked "Gifts From The Heart" Harlequin romance book, plus cash register receipts and a check or money order payable to Harlequin Gifts From The Heart Offer, to cover postage and handling.

002

CHECK ONE	ITEM	# OF PROOFS OF PURCHASE	POSTAGE & HANDLING FEE
	01 Brass Picture Frame	2	$ 1.00
	02 Heart-Shaped Candle Holders with Candles	3	$ 1.00
	03 Heart-Shaped Keepsake Box	4	$ 1.00
	04 Gold-Plated Heart Pendant	5	$ 1.00
	05 Collectors' Doll Limited quantities available	12	$ 2.75

NAME _____

STREET ADDRESS _____ APT. # _____

CITY _____ STATE _____ ZIP _____

Mail this certificate, designated number of proofs of purchase (inside back page) and check or money order for postage and handling to:

Gifts From The Heart, P.O. Box 4814
Reidsville, N. Carolina 27322-4814

NOTE THIS IMPORTANT OFFER'S TERMS

Requests must be postmarked by May 31, 1988. Only proofs of purchase from specially marked "Gifts From The Heart" Harlequin books will be accepted. This certificate plus cash register receipts and a check or money order to cover postage and handling must accompany your request and may not be reproduced in any manner. Offer void where prohibited, taxed or restricted by law. LIMIT ONE REQUEST PER NAME, FAMILY, GROUP, ORGANIZATION OR ADDRESS. Please allow up to 8 weeks after receipt of order for shipment. Offer only good in the U.S.A. Hurry—Limited quantities of collectors' doll available. Collectors' dolls will be mailed to first 15,000 qualifying submitters. All other submitters will receive 12 free previously unpublished Harlequin books and a postage & handling refund.

OFFER-1RR

PAMELA BROWNING

...is fireworks on the green at the Fourth of July and prayers said around the Thanksgiving table. It is the dream of freedom realized in thousands of small towns across this great nation.

But mostly, the Heartland is its people. People who care about and help one another. People who cherish traditional values and give to their children the greatest gift, the gift of love.

American Romance presents HEARTLAND, an emotional trilogy about people whose memories, hopes and dreams are bound up in the acres they farm.

HEARTLAND...the story of America.

Don't miss these heartfelt stories: American Romance #237 SIMPLE GIFTS (March), #241 FLY AWAY (April), and #245 HARVEST HOME (May).

HRT-1

GIFTS FROM THE HEART

from Harlequin

FREE BY MAIL With proofs of purchase
plus postage and handling

A. **Hand-polished solid brass picture frame 1-5/8″ × 1-3/8″ with
    2 proofs of purchase.**

B. **Individually handworked, pair of heart-shaped glass candle
    holders (2″ diameter), 6″ candles included, with 3 proofs of
    purchase.**

C. **Heart-shaped porcelain keepsake box (1″ high) with delicate
    flower motif with 4 proofs of purchase.**

D. **Radiant gold-plated heart pendant on 16″ chain with compli-
    mentary satin pouch with 5 proofs of purchase.**

E. **Beautiful collectors' doll with genuine porcelain face, hands
    and feet, and a charming heart appliqué on dress with 12
    proofs of purchase. Limited quantities available. See offer
    terms.**

HERE IS HOW TO GET YOUR FREE GIFTS

Send us the required number of proofs of purchase (below) of
specially marked ''Gifts From The Heart'' Harlequin books and cash
register receipts with the Offer Certificate (available in the back pages)
properly completed, plus a check or money order (do not send cash)
payable to Harlequin Gifts From The Heart Offer. We'll RUSH you your
specified gift. Hurry—Limited quantities of collectors' doll available.
See offer terms.

103R

GIFTS FROM THE HEART
ONE PROOF
OF PURCHASE

To collect your free gift by mail you must include the necessary
number of proofs of purchase with order certificate.